Off Season

A Novel of Rape, Healing, and Reconciliation

E.S. Ruete

Dedication

For Dottie, the bravest woman I never knew.

Dear reader, this is Dottie's story. This is not a story about hospital procedure, or police procedure, or the criminal justice system. Yes I know rape processing can take more than eight hours. Yes I know that most rape cases don't come to trial for two years, if at all. But every time I tried to do research and speak accurately about those topics, Dottie told me, "No. Tell my story. Tell the story of how it felt for me." This is not a story about reality. It is about the Truth that precedes and shapes reality.

Dottie is not a real person. She is just a character. But to say she came from my imagination would not be accurate either. It is more like she was in the inkwell of my Parker fountain pen, like a genie trapped in a bottle, and I simply released her.

She brought with her the other players in her story. Each character told me her or his story in their own words, but none with the urgency, the sadness, or the courage of Dottie.

No woman chooses to be raped. I asked Dottie why she chose to tell me a story of rape. She said that millions of women, hundreds every day, have stories of rape that never get told. She told her story because she could. Because she had to. Because maybe people would hear in a work of fiction a Truth that they could not hear in any other way.

TABLE OF CONTENTS

ACKNOWLEDGMENTS

This is my book. I wrote it, typed it, edited it, proofed it, and published it. Any issues and errors I cannot blame on anyone but myself. However, I would be remiss if I did not acknowledge those who had a hand in its creation.

The Reverend Doctor John Nelson challenged me to write three dimensional characters. Anne Lamott, through a passage in *Bird by Bird* and Erica Jong, by the underlying conceit of *Any Woman's Blues* and through an in-person conversation comparing that conceit to Lamott's advice, taught me *how* to write characters that are not flat: you let the characters tell the story.

My friend and mentor, Judith Katz, told her story of rape and healing in *No Fairy Godmothers, No Magic Wands: Healing Process After Rape*. Her story is not Dottie's story, but Judith appears on page 37 and her wisdom, spirit, and courage run throughout the book.

Richard LaPorta, a professional book publisher, and I came to a mutual agreement to not work together. However, in the negotiation process, he generously shared several key insights on style and design that are incorporated in this text.

My wife, Doris Beebe, read some early chapters of Dottie's story and asked to hear from some of the men, to find out why they did it. That wish is reflected in several chapters. But more importantly, she has put up with me running off to my home office for endless hours while this book has become a reality. Thank you, my love.

1 ALL SAINTS DAY

For all the saints who from their labors rest

Glenda closed the lid on her laptop and gave an involuntary sigh of relief. All Saints Day. The First of November. The day after Halloween. The season was officially "off." The last leaf peeper had checked out four hours ago.

Not that her work had ended. She would still be busy seven days a week with maintenance and upkeep, planning, shopping, perfecting new recipes, payroll, accounting, taxes. She would be playing Innkeeper and Hostess to the people who aren't interested in Tanglewood or fall colors but just want to get away for a weekend to a quiet setting with comfy rooms and a good breakfast served at a leisurely pace.

Still it was time to switch from busy season activities and chaos to off season pace and routine, and the first order of business was to start gaining back some of the weight she had lost in the five months since Memorial Day. A trip to the Berkshire Mountain Bakery would be a good start. She might even go on to Taft Farms.

Her friends wondered why she bothered, especially the ones who were having the most difficulty controlling their middle-aged spread. "Why would anyone who looks so svelte want to gain weight?" they would ask. She tried to explain it to them. She tried to tell them how the busy season was worse than anorexia, how the weight loss was uncontrollable, but they never got it. They kept telling her she was crazy.

Until one year she believed it. She kept the weight off, although no one could tell. She was cold all winter, and had to wear so many sweaters and sets of long johns that she looked heavier than ever.

When the summer came, she didn't maintain her weight. It started to drop off again, just like every year, just as her smarter self had told her it would. When she wound up in the hospital in September, she vowed she would never try that again. She also vowed that she would never let herself think her friends knew better than she. She knew she would be spectacularly unsuccessful in keeping that latter promise to herself.

After Taft farms, she'd head home and start catching up with her Dottie who was a docent at the Rockwell Museum. Dottie kept telling Glenda she was too old to keep up this pace and it was time to find a buyer for the Fergusson B&B. Glenda had always said she was going to sell when she hit 60, but that was five years ago. She was on Medicare now, for cripes sake, and so was Dottie. What was she waiting for? Every year it took a little farther into the off season to recover from the busy season. Every year a few more of her "regulars" failed to come back. Sometimes they wrote to tell her they just couldn't make the trip anymore. Sometimes one wrote to say they couldn't bear to make the trip without their loved one. All too often she never heard anything.

Still every year there were new faces, new people to meet, potential regulars to be courted and wooed and turned into friends she would see every year. She was like the college coach that hated to retire before she saw her recruits graduate – and who kept recruiting every year. The new faces were starting to count on Glenda, to look forward to her particular brand of hospitality.

But Dottie counted on Glenda, too. Dottie was cutting back her hours at the museum. Didn't Glenda have a way to do that? Couldn't she give Dave a lot more responsibility and hire an assistant manager to take up the slack? She didn't have to sell, did she? Well, yes, she probably did. Hiring another manager, even an assistant, would drastically reduce her take from the Fergie. She couldn't afford to semi-retire. When she could not keep carrying her share it would be time to sell and invest in an IRA.

But not this year.

2 THANKSGIVING

[November] I give thanks that you belong to me

Dottie was cooking Thanksgiving dinner. That was a tradition. Glenda was an excellent cook, albeit she did specialize in breakfasts, but after a long season of cooking 15 to 30 breakfasts every day, she needed a break. Early on they had fallen into the pattern of Dottie doing Thanksgiving, and she was getting pretty good at it. The menu was always the same, turkey with all the trimmings, plus a few of their particular favorites and some popular local variations, like Loka Farms maple syrup on the yams and cranberries in the stuffing.

They never had anyone over – it was dinner for just the two of them. None of their parents were alive anymore and neither of them had ever had children. Glenda had a sister in Colorado that they saw sometimes at Christmas. As for local friends, most of them thought Glenda and Dottie were just roommates sharing a house out of financial necessity. If those friends saw how Dottie and Glenda celebrated Thanksgiving, their relationship would no longer be secret, and to change their celebration just to stay in the closet and entertain friends was frankly not worth it. They had their traditions and they weren't modifying them for anyone.

Of course, they did have friends who knew. Every relationship has challenges: rough patches that you just have to talk to someone about. It certainly wasn't going to be their pastor. They were both died-in-the-wool Methodists and their church was not a member of the Reconciling Ministries Network. In fact, it actively opposed the RMN and denounced the network's work and member churches at every opportunity.

Dottie wondered why she stayed. It's hard to belong to an organization whose *Book of Discipline* contains the phrase that the way God made you is "incompatible with Christian teaching." But she knew that the book was wrong. She knew Jesus loved her, despite what some other people thought The Bible said. Christianity, and in particular Methodist Christianity, was in her blood. It was her breath. Even though she couldn't tell you how Methodist beliefs were different from UCC or Episcopalian or Presbyterian beliefs, she knew that when she attended the Open and Affirming Church on the Hill in Lenox, it felt welcoming, but the service was all wrong. It was not how she had been taught to worship. So no, she wasn't going to come out to her pastor.

Besides, you don't run to your pastor when you and your lover fight about the breakfast dishes. You talk to your friend. Mary was her friend. Mary was also a docent at the museum. She had a doting husband, three typically active boys, and an unmistakable bisexual vibe that Dottie had sensed the first time she met her. Not that Mary or Dottie would ever cheat on their significant others, but that vibe had made Dottie bold to come out to Mary. Now they were BFFs (isn't that the term the young people used? Or is it 'besties' now? She couldn't keep up). Whenever she got frustrated with Glenda, or was feeling disconnected or out of kilter, or even wanted to talk about how to surprise Glenda on their anniversary, Mary was her sounding board, especially during Busy Season.

Even Mary, however, was not someone they could have over for Thanksgiving. For one thing, Dottie and Glenda weren't out to Doug and the boys. For another, her friends would find out and wonder why *they* were never invited. Mary understood and was busy enough with her own extended family. Mary had a saying, "Thanksgiving and Christmas are for family, Halloween and New Years are for friends."

But not having people over didn't solve the whole problem. Two women having Thanksgiving dinner together every year would be like sending up signal flares. So they had to keep it low key. Often they pretended they weren't home, drawing the front blinds, letting the phone go to voice mail, and dining by candlelight in the back of the house. The rest of the time they treated it like any other day as far as the world was concerned. Dottie bought the turkey far out of town, and added the other items to the shopping list one or two at a time all through October and November. Besides, everyone knew – even those who "knew" that they were only roommates – that Dottie and Glenda had been friends for long enough that Dottie took an active role in getting Glenda filled out for the winter and the next busy season.

They took advantage of being alone to make some of their own traditions. While each of their families had dressed up for Thanksgiving dinner when they were kids, Dottie and Glenda decidedly did not. They came to dinner in their bathrobes and fuzzy slippers – and little else. If they wore anything under their robes, it was something lacy or frilly designed to show off more than it hid. Dottie was getting a warm glow just thinking about what Glenda had found for last year. After dinner, they had a Nap with a capital "N," followed by a regular nap with a lower case "n," then watched the first of the string of Christmas movies that would take them through Advent. When it was her turn to choose Glenda usually picked *Miracle on 34th Street* because the story started with the Macy's Thanksgiving

Day Parade, and that seemed an appropriate way for Dottie and Glenda to kick off their Christmas season. Glenda liked watching a movie that started off with the holiday that she and Dottie were celebrating.

But this year it was Dottie's turn to choose. She was going to surprise Glenda. Instead of *White Christmas*, her usual choice, she was going with *Love, Actually*... She liked all the different expressions of love, and she really didn't mind Glenda checking out the hotties in Billy Mack's backup band.

This year, after dinner and The Nap, they didn't bother robing up again for the nap and the movie. The fire was warm, and the day unseasonably so.

Just when Hugh Grant and his Bobbie were searching the dodgy end of town for Natalie, they heard what sounded like a branch snapping. Dottie turned and thought she saw a face disappear from the window. They heard a vehicle start up and drive out of their driveway. They paused the movie, threw on coats and boots, and went out to investigate. There were footprints in the November mud leading from the driveway around the house, pausing at the window then running back to the driveway – Dottie had noticed that there were many more and much deeper prints by the window and the prints headed away had a much longer stride than the ones coming from the front.

Glenda made a joke about being in love with Sherlock Holmes. She was all for ignoring it, but she hadn't seen the face. It kept Dottie awake half the night. Good thing she didn't have a Friday shift at the museum. She couldn't get that pasty white vision out of her mind.

3 BLACK THURSDAY

Now the first of December was covered with snow
And so was the turnpike from Stockbridge to Boston

Dottie woke up wondering where she was and why she was so cold. The first thing she noticed was that she must be outside – she was lying on cold ground and snow was hitting her in unusual places.

That's when she noticed the second thing. Her skirt was pulled up past her waist and her panties were gone. And the third thing. Her pussy hurt. *God damn those fuckers.* It started to come back to her.

She had been in Lenox having coffee in a café. She had avoided the wine bar at *The Bookstore* because the name, *Get Lit*, while a great pun, was something that a certain element in town had started taking too literally. (Ow. In her condition that unintended pun really hurt.)

She tried to see if she could sit up. Nothing seemed broken, and the bruising seemed to all be between her legs. They must have slipped something into her coffee. Small blessing. At least she had been in no shape to resist – who knows what they might have done to her, how they might have hurt her, if she'd been awake and fighting. A scene from *The General's Daughter* flashed in her mind. If they had

9

stripped her naked and tied her down, in this weather she'd be dead for sure.

So avoiding *Get Lit* had become her routine. She resented having to do that, because usually it was such a nice place. Instead, she went to the café around the corner. Apparently not far enough around the corner. Damn. What they gave her must have been roofies. She was having trouble remembering. There were three of them – no, maybe four. Even though the café was crowded with tables, they had wanted to dance with her. To Appalachian hammered dulcimer. They *must* have been lit.

She stood up, pushed down her skirt, and looked to see what she had going for her. She couldn't believe it! There was her purse, with her wallet and cell phone intact. The gall. The *egotism*! They so believed that they would convert her, that she would enjoy it, that she would be glad for the experience, they not only left her alive, they left her the means of rescuing herself! If her phone had a signal.

Somehow they had figured out she was gay. She might never call herself "lesbian" again. Not after the way it had sounded when they taunted her, over and over and over. "Come on, lesbian, you probably never had a man!" Which was true. For all her time with Glenda, she had still been technically a virgin. Which accounted for the patch of blood on the snow where she had just been lying. Someone had broken her hymen.

"Come on, dance with me! I'll show you what real love is!" How had they known? Some would say it was her clothes, but bulky sweaters, woolen maxi skirts, and Birkenstock sandals with heavy wool socks were the uniform for women of a certain group and a certain age in the Berkshires in December, gay or straight. Wait. That sound and face on Thanksgiving. Could that have been one of them?

She and Glenda had tried so hard to keep their status to themselves. They hadn't even gotten married when Massachusetts passed the first marriage equality law in the

U.S. They were proud of their state, but they were still very selective about who they came out to. (To whom they came out? Ow! Her head *really* hurt. She didn't need to be correcting her own grammar at a time like this.)

That must have been when it happened. One of them had pulled her out of the chair and started to dance with her. In the time it had taken to pull away, slap him, and sit down to her coffee, one of the others must have put something in it.

She couldn't remember much after that (*where did I hear that rohypnol does that to you?*) but she'd heard the tales and seen the reenactments. She must have seemed overcome by something. Perfect gentlemen that they were, they helped her on with her coat, picked up her purse (*thank goodness*) and helped her to their waiting car. More likely a pickup truck. Now, no time to be going all stereotype. She knew a lot of men with pickup trucks who would never do something like this. Hell, she even knew some women with pick 'em ups.

Thankfully she was too old to get pregnant. *Stop that! Stop minimizing! There is nothing good about this situation! I've been raped, probably multiple times. With no evidence of any condoms. Shit, you're never too old to get an STD.*

First thing I've got to get out of here, get a rape kit, get a blood test for roofies, get tested. God, her head hurt. *I wonder if I have cell coverage here. I wonder where "here" is?* She looked around. She knew this place! The campground at October Mountain! She was up the closed road, almost to the end. There were the camping yurts! Not that she and Glenda were campers, but they liked to take walks here.

Two bars. Probably enough. She punched 911. Didn't cell towers give priority to 911? If they didn't, they should. All available cells should be straining to pick up emergency calls. Like a cat up a tree or a neighbor playing their music too loud. She would never again even make jokes about people misusing 911. Now that she knew what a real emergency is.

"Hello, 911 operator, what is the nature of your emergency?"

"I've been raped and left in October Mountain State Forest. I'm near the yurts in the campground at the corner of Woodland Road and Willow Road. I can get the latitude and longitude off my phone if you need it." If she could keep focus long enough.

"Are you injured?"

"Not seriously, but I'm getting really cold, and my concentration comes and goes."

"We'll send an ambulance right away."

"I need to get to a hospital where they can do a rape kit and test for STDs and rohypnol."

"Understand. Your name?"

"Dorothea Conklin."

"Okay, Ms. Conklin. We have a female officer nearby in a cruiser. She has experience with these cases. Would you like me to send her instead of the ambulance?"

There might be male EMTs on the ambulance. She didn't want to write off half the human race, but...Yes; she did. At least for now. "Yes, please send her and cancel the ambulance."

"Alright, Ms. Conklin." Important to give the victim choices. She had just survived having all choice taken away. Putting her back in control as soon as possible put her on the road to healing. "I can have someone from the Sexual Assault Crisis Center meet you at the hospital. Would you like that?"

"Yes, please."

"Okay, Officer Johnson is on her way. Stay on the phone with me until she arrives." *Okay, I'm not giving the victim a choice, but this is more important than choice. She needs to know she's not alone and I need to know that she's still conscious – that she's still alive.* "Can you tell me what happened?"

"Is that really a good idea? What if I end up contradicting myself? I'm not real clear right now."

"I need to know if you have any information for putting out an APB for the attacker."

"Attackers, I think. They put something in my coffee at the café in Lenox. There were three or four of them taunting me. I don't remember much after that. I would guess they were all involved, but I really don't know. It would have taken a lot of them to carry me up this road from the locked gate. Or a pretty good off-road four-by to get over the gully from the parking lot. Say, how is the police lady going to get to me? Should I start walking to the gate?"

"No, just stay where you are. I've contacted State Forest to get the gate open. If they don't get there first, Officer Johnson has bolt cutters. You just stay where you are. She'll get to you. She'll need a minute to secure the scene, then as soon as backup is there you'll be on your way."

"I hope her cruiser is warm."

"I'll alert her to crank up the heat. She should be getting close."

"Yes, I hear a siren. I guess that's her. In fact, more than one. It sounds like we won't have to wait long for backup. Just ask them to let her come alone first. I'm not ready to see men right now."

"I understand. I'll do what I can." This lady was going to need some time to recover. Some time and some help. "Stay with me, Ms. Conklin."

"Dottie. You can call me Dottie."

"Okay, stay with me Dottie. How are you doing?"

"I'm so tired and my head hurts. And I'm so cold. I'm going to go sit on the front porch of a yurt. It seems to be out of the wind and the snow a little bit."

"Don't fall asleep on me now. You can sit down but don't lie down. Which yurt is it?"

"I don't know. Oh, wait, here's the sign. Yurt C. The one farthest down the hill."

"Okay, keep talking to me until Officer Johnson gets there."

"She's here. The car just pulled up. I see her getting out. I'm so tired…"

Most of the rest was a blur. She had some vague recollection of a police woman helping her to the car, a conversation about whether she wanted to sit in front and be close or stretched out in the back – apparently she had chosen the front seat for the warmth and for the security of having a heavily armed woman that close. She didn't remember much of the ride to the hospital, or the processing.

Mostly what she remembered is that they kept giving her choices. Blood or vaginal exam first. Left or right arm for the blood draw. Keep her clothes or change into the comfortable, impersonal sweats the SACC counselor had brought. Should they call her church. She tried to appreciate what they were trying to do. *But I'm so tired,* she thought, *and still a little cold and god my headache is getting worse. And all these decisions don't help. Didn't I hear something on NPR about decision fatigue? Or something like that.*

She remembered a book from her youth. *The Captain.* The new skipper of an ocean-going tugboat couldn't handle all the arbitrary decisions, so he just alternated "yes" and "no" answers. It seemed to work for him. She tried it.

"Do you want soup?"

"Yes."

"Do you want coffee?"

"No."

"Do you want us to call someone at your church?"

"Yes." *Damn!! Did I just say that? I love those judgmental bitches, but they're the last people I need to see right now.*

She wasn't doing much better when Mandy showed up and said all the wrong things. How could this happen? Why weren't you more careful? Are you sure you weren't at some level asking for it?

"NO! Why the hell would I ask for this? I don't even like men!" *SHIT! shit shit shit shit shit shit shit.* She just outed herself to her church. She had a feeling the rape was going to start all over again.

4 OFFICER JOHNSON

The Berkshires seemed dreamlike on account of that frostin'

There was one black and white already at the gate when I arrived. They had gotten there two minutes before me – just enough time for them to get out the bolt cutters, get the lock off the gate, and get the gate open so they could wave me through. They brought me up to date on the radio so I didn't have to slow down to talk to them. They were standing by to secure the crime scene as soon as I had the alleged victim safe and on her way to the hospital.

I didn't see any tracks as I went up the hill. I didn't know the new Hemi Dodge as well as the old Crown Vic, didn't know how it would handle the fresh powder, so I had to be a little cautious. If I didn't have a subject potentially suffering from exposure and frostbite and a crime scene getting dusted with the wrong kind of dust, I would have chained up, but that would take longer than a little caution on a quarter of a mile of hill.

I found Ms. Conklin – Dottie, she said – where the dispatcher had said I would, on the porch of Yurt C. I took a moment to put on plastic gloves and grab a large evidence bag. If roofies had been involved, there was a good chance the perps had handled her purse as they helped her out of the café and I wanted to get it bagged and tagged for the investigation.

She was pretty much incoherent by the time I found her. She was pretty clear that she wanted to be as close to me and the heater as she could get, and she kept reaching for the shotgun but not quite touching it. She didn't seem like she really wanted to do anything with it, she didn't seem to be the type to have much to do with weapons – but trauma like that on top of roofies can take you to a place you usually don't like to go. I didn't discourage her too much, even though she isn't supposed to touch it. What was it that shrink back at the Academy said? 'There's power in the shadow zone,' which I guessed to be that dark place where you don't want to go. Well, she was already in a dark place where she didn't want to be. She was going to need all the power she could find in there to get her out. So I let her reach for it. I was pretty sure she was never going to touch it.

I was sweating by the time we reached the hospital. I'd kept the heater going full blast the whole way because Dottie didn't seem to be warming up very quickly. I didn't give her the blanket I had in back because I knew the air in the cruiser was warmer than what was trapped in her clothes. In fact, I tried to get her to take off her coat and let the warmth in. If she'd been just a little more blue around the lips, I would have said screw preserving the evidence, stripped us both down to our skivvies, and wrapped us up so my body heat could get her warm. If the creeps – sorry, alleged creeps – had left her any skivvies.

The snow was already making the driving dicey. I finally got behind a snowplow, positioned myself just back of the pattern from his salt spreader, and followed him all the way down Rte. 7 to Fairview. Dottie and I were both in a hurry, but it wouldn't do us much good to wind up in a ditch.

I kept up with the radio chatter. The boys back at October Mountain had found what appeared to be the actual crime scene. They got tape up and put a tent over it so the snow wouldn't cover things up any more than it already had. They didn't find any tracks in the snow on the road besides mine, so they picked a spot and dug a channel across to see if there was any packed snow or ice trails underneath. They didn't find any. Bad because we couldn't get tread impressions. Good because it helped fix the time of the incident. They must have cleared out before it started snowing. Besides, they did find tracks where a four-by had crossed the gully, and were working on getting plaster casts of those tread marks. The mud pattern indicated the vehicle had gone up the road to the crime scene. So we had the tires and we had a latest time.

By the time we got to Fairview, Dottie's teeth weren't chattering – quite so much. I knew it might be a critical time. As she warmed up and the drug began to lose its grip on her, she might begin to remember things. I started sharing my attention between the radio and anything Dottie might say – anything to help the case, any way to help her, anything to start her healing.

Geez, you never get used to this. I've never been in her Birkenstocks, so I can't even imagine what it must be like to be inside her skin. It must be crowded in there, with her and the man or men who were inside her uninvited. Later, she would try and wash them off, but it wouldn't work. They weren't on her skin, the were under it.

I know that much because I've seen it before, way too many times. They always wanted a woman to pick them up, and most of the time that was me. It seems like I've been getting called for this duty a lot lately – enough that I begin to wonder if we have a serial rapist on our hands.

But the M.O.s are always different, except for the drugs. Where they met their attacker, what they were drinking, where they were when they woke up, demographics of the victim, even how much they had been undressed and level of abuse didn't seem to follow any pattern. The only thing they had in common was the lab found rohypnol, if we tested their blood in time. Maybe it wasn't one or more serial rapists. Maybe it was a new 'pharmacist' in town. Maybe someone was selling the stuff. Never too much to any one customer for them to get hooked on it, get caught, let us trace it back to the dealer. Smart.

"Officer?"

"Susan."

"Susan, are we getting any closer?"

"We're almost there. Just a few more minutes. They're waiting for you. The SACC counselor is there, and they've got a gurney with heated blankets by the door and more blankets in the oven." *In the oven – was that a bad expression to use with a rape victim?* "The doctor with the rape kit is standing by, and so is the phlebotomist to take your blood."

"I'm so cold."

But she's getting warmer or she wouldn't have started to talk.

"I guess that's a good sign. When you picked me up I was too cold to feel it. They say freezing to death is a pleasant way to go. I was starting to look forward to it. More than I am to this."

"They'll make it as easy as they can, and go as fast or as slow as you want. The crisis counselor will explain everything to you before they do anything, and you don't have to do any of it if you don't want to. Except warm up. We're not allowed to let you freeze to death no matter how nicely you ask."

"No, I want to do it. I want to help you find these…men! and put them away."

"It won't be easy. Can you remember anything that might help?"

"There were three or four of them. It's so hard to re-member. The place was full of men, and they were all in uniform: flannel shirt, jeans, muddy boots, and a ball cap that said, 'Shoot, Bubba, let's go kill something.' I stole that joke from Brett Butler. But something in that image seems wrong. I think there was one guy with a cowboy hat and a belt buckle the size of a dinner plate.

"And really fancy boots. I remember noticing the boots before things started getting ugly. Yeah, boots, buckle, big hat. He was there. He was in on it. He was the guy that pulled me out of my chair to dance. And that's the last thing I remember."

It wasn't much, but I would put it in my report, my report that I could practically cut and paste from the last seven. Maybe we'd get somewhere on this one.

5 SHERI

With ten miles behind [her] and ten thousand more to go

I'm getting to know this emergency room too well, and they're getting to know me. They don't even ask for my credentials any more. We're on a first-name basis. They just wave me through and tell me what cubicle they're going to put the alleged victim in. Alleged – what a joke. I'll admit that sometimes my sisters – God love them – do change their minds and cry 'rape.' But very few of those cases wind up here. I've never seen one that is even close. I wish some of the people on those juries, some of those judges, could see what I see. No, I don't wish that on anyone. I wish no one ever had to see what I see. I especially wish the 'alleged' victim didn't have to see it, didn't have to go through it, but it still bothers me that, in spite of all we do to document and collect evidence, people in court never quite see things the same way I do.

Okay, first to get any info the staff has. Probably not much yet.

"Officer Johnson is bringing her in."

Susan. Good. She's a good officer, and a good person. She'll take care of her. She's got experience. Too much, just like me.

"The dispatcher says they're about ten minutes out. Slow going in this snow. The victim told 911 that she'd been drugged, raped, and left in October Mountain. She suspected multiple attackers, but says she slept through the whole thing. That's about all. Officer Johnson says she's still in and out. Suffering from exposure and probably frostbite in the extremities. That's all we know."

Enough. Enough to get started. Time to go through my mental checklist. I try to keep it all in my head; it's way too clinical and not empathic enough if I stand here with a clipboard ticking off items, and yet I don't want to forget anything. I probably couldn't, I've been doing this so much lately, but my father-in-law once told me that most plane crashes happen when the pilot has about 200 hours of flight time – when they think they know what they're doing and get cocky. I don't want to get cocky. So let's review.

Vaginal exam, swab for attacker's DNA, cheek swab for victim's DNA so it can be eliminated during tests. Pictures of injuries. All the other little – and big – indignities of the rape kit. Forensic evidence can take hours. None of it my job, but explaining it all *is* my job. That and getting okays from the vic – she's in charge. The nurses and I are pretty good at figuring out whether they should get the permission slips signed or I should. Sometimes she will trust me more. Sometimes it's the same problem of the clipboard getting in the way of just being there for her. We play it by ear.

What else medical? Out of the usual? Warm her up, treat her for frostbite. Got to ask the nurse details about how they do that so I can share them with the vic. Wish I had a name. I hate calling her 'a vic.' And blood tests – the usual for STDs and pregnancy – I wonder if she's fertile – and this time extra vials for drugs. I'll have to ask how many. I hope it's not overwhelming. These phlebotomists are angels, but nobody likes having that needle just stay in their arm, even those who aren't cold and traumatized.

I've got the sweat suits. Four sizes. Waif, normalish, Rubenesque, morbidly obese. That last is the hardest to fit. If you're beyond moderately overweight, you get the size big enough for a lineman for the Patriots. Bigger, actually. I've got my own little magic trick. Makes me think of that card trick where once the magician knows your card they know which envelope to pull out of which pocket to reveal that card. I never let them know I have sweats in any other sizes than the one I pull out for them. Makes it more personal. Like they're normal, and they wear the same thing everybody else does. Got to make them feel normal. Once she walks in I'll make the call, put them in my tote, leave the others at the nurses' stand.

Now my stuff. Got my card. Several of them: enough for friends and family if there are any. Pamphlets for the Sexual Assault Crisis Center: check. That's mostly for the significant other or BFF if they show. Too much too soon for the vic.

Assess her state. Assess her level of trauma. Assess her level of consciousness. With roofies she may have trouble staying focused. I've seen a lot of that lately.

Assess her level of vulnerability. How many people can she handle? How many bright lights? Or is she afraid of the dark? How many men? Zero is often a good number to start with, but Dr. Patel is on duty tonight. We work well together. We should. We've done it enough times. He's small, gentle, in touch, empathic. Moderate. A good bridge back to the world.

Then tomorrow. Follow-up call. Time will depend on what time we get out of here tonight, who's going to take her home, how long it's going to take in this snow, an assessment of whether she'll go straight to bed or stay up talking half the night. With roofies, probably the first, but you never know. Noon is probably a good first guess. They usually want to get up for lunch. For a long time she'll be too traumatized to have much interest in food, but by lunch time hunger often rears its head.

Hook her up with a counselor. One of the good ones. One who knows the difference between integrating trauma and curing neuroses. God, the damage those psychologists can do. I hate this part of the checklist. Every time I think about therapists this comes up for me. I get pulled…

"Sheri, you keep telling the same story over and over. You're fixating. You have to let it go."

"I can't let it go. It's right in front of my eyes every second. I know it wasn't my fault, but I can't help feeling that it was stupid to go anywhere near that party."

"What I hear you saying is that you feel it's your own fault for going to a party that wasn't safe."

"Yeah, I guess it was. They told us at orientation to be careful about that. I guess I should have listened."

"Now we're getting somewhere. You can't change what you are until you take responsibility for your own actions."

What an idiot. It took me years to get over the damage he did in that 'support' group. Support my ass. That's why I try to get good counselors for my girls. Like this woman coming in now. She'll be here any second now. Time to go to work. They're rolling out the gurney. I guess she won't be walking in. There's the lights from the squad car. God, it's really snowing out there. Hell of a way to start the month. Looks like the number three sweats.

"White female, name is Dorothea Conklin. Goes by 'Dottie.' Exposure, frostbite in a few digits. Sexual trauma. Appears to have been drugged. In and out of consciousness. Complaining of headache. No lacerations or contusions. Medicare with AARP supplemental insurance. Let's get those blankets on her and start treating those fingers and toes."

"Hi, Ms. Conklin, may I call you Dottie? I'm Sheri Kaplan, an advocate from the Sexual Assault Crisis Center. They're going to treat you for frostbite and check you for injuries before we address the sexual assault. Is that okay? I'll be with you the whole time, explaining each step and getting your permission before they do anything. Is that okay? You don't have to do anything you don't want to, you don't have to do anything until you're ready. Okay? You let me know what you want me to do. I can hold your hand, I can rub your head, I can just stay close or go stand in a corner or leave the room or go home. You let me know what you want me to do."

She's not saying much, but the left hand, the one with no frostbite, is reaching for me. I'll just hold that and watch her. Those eyes. They're all different, and they're always the same. Terrified. It's still happening, and the future is starting to push in, too. She has no idea what it's going to be like, but deep down she can feel it's not going to be good.

She's going to have to tell her story, over and over, until she becomes comfortable with the fact that it's her story, a part of her.

"This is bullshit."

"Now Sheri, we don't use that language here."

"The fuck we don't. 'Bullshit' is a lot less dangerous than the language you're using. Telling me that it was my fault, that I wanted it, that I probably enjoyed it. You weren't there. You didn't have some asshole jock sitting on your belly holding your nose while he poured liquor down your throat. You didn't feel him tear your shirt open and grind his thumbs into your tits, rubbing your nipples raw. You didn't have your pants ripped off. You didn't get raped. And raped and raped and raped."

"Now Sheri, talk like that doesn't help anyone."

"It helps me."

"No, it doesn't. You're fixating again. To recover ..."

"Recovery, hell. You've never lost anything that you didn't buy, nothing you couldn't replace as soon as you got the insurance check. You don't recover from what Amelia lost, what I lost, what everyone in this room has had taken from them in one way or another. This is bullshit. You're bullshit."

"You tell him, Sheri."

"Yeah, you go, girl!"

"Now everybody let's calm down. We were getting somewhere

with Sheri. We were getting to the root of her issues."

"No, we weren't. You were. The girl was raped. Rape is not an issue. It's not an obsession or compulsion or neurosis you recover from. It's not an addiction that you are in recovery from. It's not something you own, it's something that owns you. It's a violation. It's a big gaping wound. If you're lucky you survive it and it heals over, but it leaves a scar that is always there. You don't recover from it. You don't even get to the place where you say you're in recovery. You just is. 'Raped' is a part of you the rest of your life. But you wouldn't know about that, you tight-assed little white male fucker..."

"Sheri?"

"Yes, Dottie."

"Where did you go?"

"Nowhere, I've been right here, holding your hand."

"But your eyes went away. They were watching me. Then they weren't. They were in the distance. Where were you? What were you looking at?"

"I was looking at my past. And your future. With you. Thinking of what you're going to face, and resolving that you won't have to face it alone. I'll be there whenever you need or want me to be."

"Can I go to sleep now?"

"Yes. I'll stay right here. I'll make sure we wake you if anything changes or it's time for the next step."

"Keep holding my hand?"

"Yes, if you want."

"It's okay if your eyes go away, as long as you keep holding my hand."

"I'll hold your hand." From the emergency room to the courtroom. You have a long journey ahead, and you've only just begun.

6 THE GRAPEVINE

There's...A song that they sing of their home in the sky
Maybe you can believe it if it helps you to sleep

The little slut. I knew it. I knew there was something off about her. About both of them. 'Sharing' a house. Just 'roommates.' *Way* too convenient. Abomination! Unclean! Both of them! That's the problem with the world today – we're not allowed to stone people like that. Maybe that Moslem Sahara law stuff wouldn't be so bad, if those Mohamadans weren't such heathen pagans. They at least know how to handle sinners. How could they darken the door of our church for so many years?

I have got to get on the phone *right away* and marshal the troops. Marshal, what an interesting word. Like the guy who used to organize the posse. Or the lynch mob. No, I guess the Marshal was always trying to stop the lynch mob. Fair trial first. Then punishment. Well, we don't need any more trial. She confessed right in front of me. As good as came right out and said 'I'm a flaming, Godless, God-dammed lesbian and I come to church with my devil lover right under your noses, and I'm going to rub them in it.' The nerve, saying that to me, when I was there trying to help.

And of course she was asking for it. Her sicko lifestyle is a choice she made, but somewhere inside the real woman wanted to be rescued, be converted. She was sending signals to this guy the whole time she was protesting that she didn't want it. Didn't want it my eye. Of course she wanted it. Even if her eggs are dried up, that old maternal instinct is still there, that old find-the-right-man-to-be-the-father-of-my-babies feeling is still strong, must have been exuding all over wherever it was that she picked him up.

Oh, yes, she picked *him* up, hadn't you heard? They? Date rape drug? No way, who have you been listening to? I got this straight from Laurie Ann, who got it straight from Sarah Jane, who got it from Louise, who got it straight from Mandy, who talked to her *in the hospital.* Mandy is the one Dottie came out to! Oh, she was all confused, finally seeing that Lesbian was a choice and she didn't want to choose that anymore and so she picked up this guy at a biker bar, but then she didn't want to tell Glenda so she cried, 'Rape!'

And then she tried to get cozy with that handsome young policeman – the one we just hired straight out of the Academy – on the way to the hospital. Susan Johnson? Of course not! Who have you been listening to? I got this straight from Martha who got it straight from Laurie Ann.

Well, Sarah Jane told me that Martha told her that Dottie had them burn her slutty clothes that she bought to entice the guy so Glenda wouldn't see them.

No, it wasn't Dottie that got raped, it was Glenda. She was bragging about what a great Lesbian she was, and what a great lesbian lover she had, and how no man could ever satisfy a woman the way a woman wanted to be satisfied, and how they were really pulling the wool over the eyes of our church and *dared* the boys to do something about it and so they did, they pulled the wool over *her* eyes – they pulled that lesbo wool skirt right up over her head and fu…well, you know what they did and serves her right.

No, it was definitely Dottie, Glenda doesn't wear skirts,

she wears jeans or khakis. I feel bad for Dottie, for both of them, but it was certainly God's punishment for all the years of lying and sneaking and sinning and whoring. Well, I heard a young woman preach a sermon on the Prodigal Son and she said that parable was all about giving mercy and letting God take care of meting out justice. No, we can't let them off the hook, of course not, I'm just saying...

Excommunicate them? Do Methodist's do that? I heard about that case where they put a pastor on trial for performing a gay marriage for his son, but I never heard of it for a lay person, no matter who they lay with. Oh, stop it, it wasn't that clever. Well, I just don't know how we get them out of the church. There must be some way. We all stood up and agreed to let them join, can't we just stand up and say we don't want them anymore?

We just make it too uncomfortable for them to be around. Just give them the silent treatment. Don't pass the peace with them. Messages from the pulpit. Prayer cards with very pointed messages. They have a name for it at West Point. The Amish call it shunning. They are dead to me.

Well, I think we should have an emergency meeting of the Methodist Women Christian Charity Circle and figure out a strategy that we can all use. I'll call Mandy, as President she should pick the time, but I definitely think it should be before Sunday so we know what to do when – and if – they show up for services.

7 THE CALL

It's by far the hardest thing I've ever done
To be so in love with you and so alone

Dottie, where the hell are you? I don't know whether to be angry or scared – or both. Or numb. It's not that big a deal. It's only supper, but it's not like Dottie. No supper no note no call no text. Not that Dottie would text. Her car's not here. That's when I first started getting sick to my stomach. Why would her car not be here? I don't know if my stomach is hurting because it's hungry, or because I'm angry, or because I'm on the edge of panic. I don't think it's hunger, but I don't even remember getting out this box of crackers I've been munching on. Who can I call? Who would understand my worry without figuring out more than I, we, want them to know? Mary hasn't heard from Dottie since their shift was over at one o'clock. I can't call the police until it's been 24 hours. I wish I knew someone on the force I could call and just ask them to keep an eye out for Dottie's car. Who was that officer on the Lenox force who used to like my scones and would keep an eye on the Fergusson for a cup of coffee? I haven't seen him around in years. He must have gotten too old – or else I did. He certainly never knew he was wasting his time. I'll go out and drive around a bit. If Dottie calls, she has my cell number. But where do I start? What if she comes home while I'm out looking? Then she'll worry about me. No, I'm better staying here.

31

Especially with the snow they're predicting. It's just starting to fall. I better stay put.

"Hello, Ms. Eastwick? This is Sheri Kaplan from the Sexual Assault Crisis Center. I'm here at Fairview hospital with…"

"Is it Dottie? Is she okay?"

"Yes, it's Ms. Conklin. She's here being treated for exposure and frostbite in one finger and two toes, but she's going to be fine."

"Can I see her? When is she coming home? Can I talk to her?" *Am I saying too much? Do I sound like more than just a concerned roommate? How much did Dottie say?*

"She's busy with the doctor right now. They've drawn some blood, warmed her up, treated her fingers and toes. Now they're checking her for any other health concerns, then they'll look for evidence of assault." She had to stop herself from saying "rape kit."

"So it was rape." Glenda wasn't going to mince any words – call a spade a spade. No niceties here. Best to confront reality from the beginning.

"It appears so. She is having trouble remembering. Some of the blood they drew is to test for drugs. She has every appearance of having been given rohypnol. She thinks there were three or four men. They picked her up in the café in Lenox and dropped her in October Mountain. There is evidence that that is where the alleged assault occurred."

"Alleged assault? You mean gang bang?"

"We have to stick with 'alleged' until a jury says it really happened. We have to be very careful until then or we could jeopardize the case." *If it ever goes to trial.* Sheri knew the odds were against it.

Glenda drew an audible sigh. "Okay, I'll try to be good. I'll leave the shotgun in the closet – for now."

"*Mizz Eastwick!*"

"Just kidding. I don't even own a gun. Hate those

things. 'Shotgun' is a dirty word as far as I'm concerned. But Parade says swearing can be a needed release at a time like this."

"Okay. Now, Ms. Eastwick, were you aware that Ms. Conklin's hymen was intact until this incident?"

"You mean 'alleged incident,' don't you?"

"No, we know there was an incident. It's alleged it was not consensual. I ask again, were you aware that Ms. Conklin was a 65-year old virgin?"

"No." But it didn't surprise her. Like a lot of lesbians, Glenda had tried men before she found out that wasn't her path. Some of her lesbian friends had even married men and had children before they gave up on men in disgust. Not Dottie. Glenda thought back to the conversations she and Dottie had when they really *were* just roommates – the conversations that led them to realize how much they had in common, how much they liked each other, how much they needed each other, how much they loved each other – pretty much in that order.

Dottie said she knew she was gay long before she knew what sex was. When she was five, she and all her friends knew that boys had cooties and wanted nothing to do with them, but by eight, the other girls had one by one changed their minds. Not Dottie. She said she was always afraid of boy cooties. Well, she certainly had a good case of boy cooties now. Hopefully that was all they gave her. I guess that's what the rest of the blood was for.

"Ms. Eastwick? Are you still there?"

"Call me Glenda. Yes, I was thinking. I didn't know, but I'm not surprised."

"I'm sorry for interrupting your train of thought. I know this all will take some time to process. As I was saying, Ms. Conklin's..."

"Dottie."

Not just first name, insisting on the nick name, the familiar name, the personal name. "Dottie's recently ruptured hymen, while adding to her stress and discomfort, establishes with certainty that an incident took place. It also forestalls the stock defense that she does this kind of thing all the time. Both good for our side if we ever find the alleged assailants." *Damn. Should have said 'when.' Gave away a little of the bad odds. Maybe Ms. Eastwick didn't notice.*

Glenda noticed the 'our side.' Did Sheri mean herself and Dottie? Did she mean the prosecution? Did she mean 'all women'? Or was she including Glenda in the concerned group – like a partner? How much had Dottie said? It was time to find out. "Can I see her if I drive over? Or at least talk to her on the phone?"

"How far away are you?"

"About 20 minutes by car."

"Usually? Because make that 40 at least in this snow. She should be done with the doctor by then. She said she really wants to see you, and that she has something to tell you."

"Okay, tell Dottie I'll be right there, and to hold on." What the hell, she probably knew anyway. "And give her my love."

"I will. And I'll be here when you get here, Ms. East… – Glenda."

"Thank you, Sheri, I look forward to meeting you."

"I just wish it was under better circumstances."

Tell me about it. It's not your lover that's getting processed for rape. It's not your partner that has just been introduced to what's going to be a long time in hell. Glenda flew around the house with feet of lead. It was like those bad dreams when you're so busy getting ready but you don't seem to get any closer to being ready. Finally after about an hour and a half – the clock in the kitchen said it had only been four minutes, she'd have to get that checked – she had on her normal jeans, a flannel shirt; wool socks and sweater; parka, hat, gloves, and boots; had found the car keys, and was backing out into the worst blizzard she could remember for this early in December. Just a week ago they had been too hot with their traditional Thanksgiving fire in the fire place and now look at it. Welcome to New England.

Stop thinking about that and focus on Dottie. The heat hadn't stopped them from having that fire. They'd just had to make adjustments. Mostly to the amount of clothing. Which hadn't bothered either of them at all. Glenda got a warm feeling. She wondered how long it would be before Dottie could have that same warm feeling. *Ooops! Turn into the skid! Better let focusing on Dottie wait and focus on the driving.* Sheri was right. It took her another 3 hours – 45 minutes by the dashboard clock, it must be in cahoots with the one in the kitchen – to reach the visitor parking lot. She wanted to run in, but suspected the footing was no better than the driving and picked her way carefully between the lumps of slush.

"Can you tell me where Dorothea Conklin is?"

"Has she been admitted?"

"I don't think so. She was brought in to be treated for exposure, frostbite, and well, ah…"

"Right. The assault case. Down to emergency. The check-in nurse will tell you where she is."

Glenda didn't get Dottie's name out at Emergency check in before a young woman with milk chocolate skin and a sad smile introduced herself as Sheri Kaplan and led her down the corridor to an exam room. "The doctor is just finishing up. Ah, here he comes now. Dr. Patel, this is Glenda Eastwick, a close friend of Dottie's."

"Are you family, Ms. Eastwick?"

"Glenda is the one Dottie has been asking for. She put her name down on the release form as someone you could share medical information with. Right *above* my name. So you can say anything in front of both of us."

"Well, there's really not much to say. The extremities with the frostbite have been warmed and are responding nicely. We'd like to keep her overnight for observation on the exposure and shock, but of course that is up to her."

"Of course. I think she'll want to come with me. We share a house in Stockbridge" – still good to be careful, especially with the doctor – "but we'll leave that up to her as you say. Now, about the rest."

"Clear evidence of sexual congress. Recent rupture of the hymen. From the volume of semen, I would say at least three ejaculations, probably from different men, but we won't know that until we get the DNA results. Vaginal tearing indicates it was not gentle lovemaking. No signs of a struggle, but that is exactly what we expect if she was drugged, which appears to be the case. I'm assuming pregnancy is not an issue. We won't know about sexually transmitted diseases until all the blood work comes back."

That is *what the rest of the blood draw was for.* She had tried to put it out of her mind. How many ways could women catch AIDS from each other? *Stop it, it's not about you, it's about Dottie. If she has something, the least of your worries is avoiding catching it. You have to get her through it.* "Can I talk to her yet?"

"Yes, she should be ready any time now."

"Do you want me there or do you want to see her alone?" This was Sheri. Glenda had almost forgotten she was there. "In case you're wondering, she told me she considers you to be her next of kin."

Well, that answered that question. I wonder how many people know? I guess I'll find out.

Dottie heard the voices in the hall. She couldn't hear words, but when Dr. Patel stopped talking and she heard Sheri and Glenda conversing, she knew they would be in soon. The voices were coming closer to the door. She ached to see Glenda, to hold Glenda, to cry on Glenda's shoulder. And she would give anything in this world or the next not to have to see her, not to have to tell her what she had done.

"Let's just ask Dottie."

Damn, another decision. What was up next, yes or no? If she said "yes" now, would she end up saying "no" to going home? Or would she be saying "no" to staying for observation? Or would there be other intervening questions? *If my head is clear enough to think of all those possibilities, I guess it's time to ditch the crutch.* She found her outdoor voice. "What are you asking Dottie?"

Sheri and Glenda came in to the cubicle. "Do you want me with you when you talk to your friend?"

"Yes, for a few minutes." Moral support to get past the dreaded news. And a witness if Glenda tried to kill her. "Then I would like to be alone with her." To deal with the ache. If Glenda didn't leave with Sheri. "Come in and close the door." She got up from the bed – was it more of a gurney? – and took Glenda in her arms. The tears came without warning, and once they started the wracking sobs weren't far behind. She just clung, held on for her life, for long moments barely able to catch her breath. Was it her imagination or was Glenda not holding as tightly as she was? When she regained her voice, the sobbed words "I'm sorry" were barely audible muffled by Glenda's shoulder.

"Sorry? Don't be sorry. Sorry for what? You didn't do anything wrong."

"But I did, I did something terrible."

"No, something terrible was done to you. Those men did this all on their own. It was not you."

"No, not that. After." Her voice was steadying a little bit. She took a deep breath, let go of Glenda, grabbed for a Kleenex. Then she heard Judith's voice from the T group long ago. It's possible to breathe, talk, and cry at the same time. So she just forged ahead while she still had the courage. "Mandy from the church came to see me. She was being such a shit. You know how judgmental she can be, even when she thinks she's being helpful. I just blurted it out."

"What?" *Here it comes…*"What did you blurt out?"

"I told her I don't like men. I as much as told her I was a lesbian. She surely figured out that we're not just roommates." *There. It's out.* Why was coming out to her partner harder than coming out to Mandy? *Love, I guess. I do love her.*

More than anything.

"Oh, is that all?" God, was she saying this? IS THAT ALL! *Isn't that about the biggest thing, the worst thing?* No, she was surprised to realize. Dottie's trauma was a big thing. Dottie's potential for infection and other health risks were big things. This was a nuisance that was going to be a complication in trying to deal with their big things, and it was a thing they had done to themselves.

She thought back to *The Family and Friends Guide to Homosexuality.* The chapter on the heterosexual closet. It's hard to keep anything about yourself in the closet, even things about your friends. It limits your freedom. They were going to pay the price now for taking the easy way out. "Is that all? It's probably time. Come here, my lovely girl."

Sheri quietly let herself out as Dottie and Glenda hugged, then kissed, then hugged some more…

8 ALICE

Lean on me when you're not strong
And I'll be your friend, I'll help you carry on

The phone rang again. The name was "Douglas, Joseph." Probably Alice, another church lady. When would they get the message? Dottie and Glenda couldn't disconnect the phone, they were waiting for news from Sheri and Susan, and if they let the machine get it, the invective was worse than when they answered it. Glenda would try one more time. "Listen, bitch, we're not sorry and we're not slinking away…"

"Glenda, for God's sake shut up and listen and don't hang up. I need to talk to Dottie but I'll talk to you first. Next to surviving my rape, my son coming out to the family was the hardest thing I ever experienced. I'm on your side."

"Coming out?"

"I bet you don't know that Trevor was born Tina. He decided he was not a girl when he was four. We let him dress as a boy until he started school. Then for a year none of the other boys noticed that he always used the stalls in the boy's room. After that we had to deal with it. However, that was long ago in a city far, far away. I just want to let you know I'm on your side. I'm tired of keeping quiet, of being in *my* closet. I don't know if we can change anything but you're not alone. Now, is Dottie there?"

"I'll go see if she wants to talk to you." Glenda held the phone away and yelled. "Dottie? It's Alice from church. I know, I thought the same thing, but she's got something to say I think you might want to hear. Okay! " She uncovered the phone mouthpiece. "Alice? She'll be right here."

"Glenda, don't let her hang up when we're done. I've got some more things to say to you."

"Alice? It's Dottie. If you're here to call me a bitch and a slut like everyone else I don't want to talk to you."

"No, I'm here mostly to listen. I'm not you, and my rape was not your rape, so …"

"You were raped?"

"Yes. But my rape was not your rape, so I don't know what you're feeling or what you're going through, but I do know a couple of things about surviving assault, and I know that one thing that helps is having someone listen. So if there's anything …"

"I'm so confused." Dottie didn't let Alice finish her sentence. "So many people are telling me so many different things, that it's my fault, that it's not my fault but I still wasn't very smart. Everybody's giving me advice on how to recover – talk about it, don't talk about it, put it behind me, get mad, don't get mad."

"What do you want to do? You have to listen to yourself, and you have to know that it's a process that takes time, that you have to figure it out. And you have to know that even when you figure it out and think that you've finished some steps, you'll probably have to go back and repeat – maybe several times before you're done. Now, what do you want to do right this minute?"

"I want to talk about it."

Dottie told her story one more time. What she told Alice was no different than what she told the dispatcher, or what she told Sheri, or what she told Glenda on the way home from the hospital that night. It was no different, but it was totally different because every listener is different, and Dottie was a different Dottie every time she told it. Dottie told it many more times after this, too. She told it to friends. It became a test. Those who took it in, who took part of the burden of Dottie's experience and made it their burden, became allies. Others who could not hear it became, not adversaries, just 'the others.' But the story was always the same.

Alice said almost nothing during the telling. Not even "uh huh" or "I see," and certainly not "you poor dear" or "I know what you're feeling." She just waited for Dottie to pause and said, "I'm still here. I'm still listening." And that is the reason why this telling felt so different to Dottie. When she told Glenda, Glenda was listening too hard, caring too much, wanting too much to fix it, torn between wanting to smother Dottie and make it all go away and wanting to drop Dottie off at home and go murder those sons-a-bitches. Dottie could sense that; Glenda even muttered 'sons-a-bitches' under her breath several times on the ride home. Dottie found herself thinking, *She's not blaming me, but it's still a woman's fault. They did it because they're sons of bitches. She's laying it all on their mothers.*

Alice didn't do any of that. She didn't comment. She didn't interrupt. She didn't try to minimize or amplify on Dottie's feelings, and Dottie just let it flow.

"I'm so scared."

"Of what?"

"Of everything."

"Name it. Name your fears. You can't confront them until you know their names. Knowing a thing's name gives you power over that thing."

"Glenda. That Glenda will think I'm damaged goods and won't love me anymore. That Glenda will think I wanted it and I'm not gay anymore. That Glenda will love me too hard, hold me too close, be too scared for me. That no matter how hard we try to be the same, the fact that we have to try will make it different, and I don't want it to be different."

"I'm still here. I'm still listening."

"I'm afraid the church won't let us back in. I'm afraid I'll have to find a new congregation, a new denomination, and I'm not sure I can learn to feel the Spirit in a foreign place. I'm afraid the Spirit will find me damaged, that Jesus wont love me anymore. I'm afraid that I'll be so afraid of people, so angry at people, especially men, that I won't feel the Spirit moving in them anymore. That used to be my greatest joy – to see the Spirit in the faces of the people at the museum. I'm afraid of hating people who I'm so afraid of and angry at."

"Are you afraid of me? Do you hate me?"

"I was ready to be. I was afraid of talking to you when Glenda said you were on the phone, and I'll bet you could hear me building up to a good hate when I picked up the phone. I'm afraid you'll judge me for judging you."

"I'm still listening."

"I'm afraid I'll never be able to sleep. I'm afraid I'll never know what they really did to me, that my imagination will keep drawing more and more awful pictures to fill in what I don't know. I'm afraid I won't ever forget how it felt to wake up with the snow falling on my exposed pussy and my bare ass sticking to the frozen ground. I'm afraid... ."

"I'm still here."

"I'm afraid I won't ever stop being afraid. I'm afraid of being afraid of everything forever, of being afraid of everyone, of never wanting to go out. Oh, God, how am I ever going to be a docent again? How am I ever going to go shopping again?"

"I'm still listening."

"I think that's it."

"I'm still here."

"I'm afraid no one will listen to me. I'm afraid people will tell me it's time to be done, to get over myself. I'm afraid they'll get tired of waiting for me. I'm afraid Glenda will get tired of waiting for me. I'm afraid you'll get tired of waiting to hear the end of it."

"I'm still listening."

"I'm tired. Thank you. I never said those things before – even to myself."

"Now that you know what you're afraid of, what are you going to do?"

"I don't know. Keep facing it. Keep a journal. Make a list. Draw up a plan. Do a spreadsheet. Action items. Reading list."

"Do it all in order."

"Right."

"Wrong. Your mind, your emotions, your soul, your body won't let you do it in order. The World won't let you do it in order. You will think you're done with a step and something will snap you right back like a rubber band. When that happens, be gentle with yourself. Now, how is your support system?"

"Well, there's Glenda."

"That can be good, or great, or very bad. I want to talk to her next. Who else?"

"Mary."

"Do I know her?"

"Another docent at the museum. My pal and confidante and pretty much the only person I'm out to. Well, she was until this."

"Does she know yet?"

"No."

"Call her. Today. This morning. As soon as we're done here. Who else?"

"Well, we both know Pastor Allen and the church will be useless."

"Don't count them out. I'm part of the church. And I think Pastor Allen might surprise us yet. And who knows who else might come out of the woodwork. Or the closet."

"Who knows. Sheri and Susan, but they both have big caseloads and I'm just another statistic to them."

"You talked about action items, and I know you think you have a lot. You only have two right now. Number one: talk to everyone who loves you about what you're going through. Number two: find even more people who love you to talk to, but make sure they love you the right way. Make sure they love you enough to listen when they're uncomfortable. Make sure they don't love themselves so much that they have to fix you so they don't have to be uncomfortable. The Bible says to love your neighbor as yourself. That's not good enough. For a while you're going to need people who are willing to love you more than themselves. Now get me Glenda."

"That's number three."

"So sue me. Get her on the phone."

"Okay. Glenda? Alice wants to talk to you again."

"Hi, Alice, I was listening to Dottie's end and figured you must be about done. What did you want to say?"

"I want to give you a piece of my mind. How dare you not come out?"

"How dare you?"

"I'll give myself a piece of my mind later. Don't try and dodge the question. How dare you not come out?"

"To our church? Do you think I'm crazy?"

"Then why stay in our church if it makes you hide so many parts of you, so many things that are important to you?"

"Because our church is important, too. It's my family, and it's hard enough coming out to biological immediate family. Extended family you do very slowly. Sometimes not at all. What makes you think I have anything to come out about anyway? What have you heard?"

"It's all over the church that you and Dottie are partners. Dottie told Mandy at the hospital. Of course, the most frequently used phrase is 'lesbian slut lovers'."

"What Dottie said exactly is 'I don't even like men.' The rest is all Mandy's extrapolation."

"Okay, so come out to me. What is the truth?"

"Dottie and I are lesbian slut lovers. And partners. In every way that matters. In all the ways that Mandy will never understand."

"That's better. Now that you're out to me, I can help you connect with the community."

"What community?"

"GLB. Or LGBT. Or LGBTQIP. Or however much alphabet soup you want to pile on. At the True Colors conference, Robin goes on for a minute and a half. She throws in terms I never even heard of like 'straight so far' and 'straight for now.' But one letter that a lot of people leave off is 'A.' And that's not for asexual, and it's not for agendered, and it's the fastest growing part of our community."

"If it's not asexual, what does it stand for?"

"Ally. We allies are multiplying like rabbits. 'Straight but not narrow' is our slogan. We are becoming legion, and that's why I'm mad at you. I'm mad at Dottie, too, but mad is so much less important than other things I feel for Dottie that I'm not going to mention it to her – yet."

"Why are you so mad at me?"

"Because the greatest source of new allies is people coming out. When you know people in the community, you find out how big the community is, and how many of our expectations – like only two genders, everybody is one or the other, and that drives their identity, their expressions, and their attractions – are fallacies. It's not until you've broken those flawed molds that you're able to accept someone who would never have fit into them.

45

"When Trevor came out, I wasn't part of the community. I was only marginally aware. I was blindsided. I wanted there to be some other explanation, like peer pressure or confusion about something. It makes the denial stage much longer and the acceptance stage much harder.

"By not coming out, you've robbed some very good people of the opportunity to love and accept you and break some of their molds. Bigotry is an onion that we're given when we're children. Then we spend a lifetime peeling away the layers. When you didn't come out, you denied your church family the opportunity to peel away layers of bigotry and apathy and become allies, and you robbed the LGBT community of allies it needs."

"So why don't you come out? No one knows about Trevor, do they?"

"Pastor Allen does, and after Sunday everyone will."

"How?"

"I'm going to put in a prayer card. Trevor is going to school in North Carolina, and this HB2 thing still isn't resolved. He may have to change his dorm and his bathroom. I'm going to ask a prayer of concern for him, and sign my name, and Pastor Allen has agreed to use my name when he reads it during the Prayers of the People."

"Wow. That should start a shit storm. Why now?"

"Well, Dottie already started a shit storm. It should help take some of the attention away from you and keep the shit moving. Maybe we can even get a good flush going. Ugh. Enough of that metaphor."

"And Pastor Allen is okay with this?"

"Pastor Allen is a closet ally. Not because of family or friends. Just because of reading what Jesus says. An ally who's about ready to come out, too. Could you put in a prayer for Dottie on Sunday?"

"Why?"

"Because Mandy and her toadies have told Pastor Allen in no uncertain terms not to read any prayers from either of you. It is part of the silent treatment they plan to use to force the two of you to leave the church. That edict can't be defied without a prayer card from you."

"That doesn't seem like a very good use of a prayer card. Shouldn't we be talking to God?"

"Oh, come on. Everyone knows public prayer is about talking to people, not to God. She already knows what we're thinking before we do. Pastor wants to use your prayer card to draw the lines as a prelude to trying to move the congregation towards becoming reconciling."

"Whoa, this doesn't seem like the right way to go about it. Asking people to choose up sides. Maybe a majority will come to our side, but Mandy and her ilk will just dig in their heels. We'll divide the church, and it may never recover."

"Or maybe Mandy and her ilk will peel away some of *their* layers of bigotry. Or maybe nobody will and we'll have to get a new pastor, but don't we have to try? Don't we have to give people a chance to grow?"

"If it's bigotry, they may change. If it's faith, it's going to be a lot harder."

"I know. But what's that old saying? 'God loves you just the way you are and loves you too much to leave you that way'?"

"Mandy I'm sure thinks God loves me too much to leave me gay."

"That's not what I meant."

"I know. You meant God loves Mandy too much to leave her as a bigot, but I don't think Mandy will hear it that way."

"Maybe she'll surprise you. I already told Dottie I think a lot of people may surprise you."

"You surprised me."

"I hope so."

"But I don't hold out much hope for Mandy, and if we don't get her, a lot of people are going to have to choose to back the Pastor or her."

"But the only other choice is for you and Dottie to

leave the church and Trevor and me to stay in the closet."

"Aren't we being selfish, talking about tearing apart the church just for the convenience of the four of us?"

"What if it's more? What if there is a whole unformed and unrecognized LGBT community at our church? And in the community at large, unchurched because they aren't accepted? What about them?"

"What would Jesus do? We have to start by loving. That's the only way we can hope to keep this from tearing the church apart. We have to love Mandy just the way she is, too."

"And too much to leave her that way?"

"I guess that's the clincher. If God loves our church too much to leave us this way, She'll guide us. But what if God is just a metaphor, just a convenient way to talk about the divine spark in each of us that helps us live together, take care of one another, and take care of the Earth? What if God has no physical presence, no ability to physically affect the physical realm?"

"Then we rely on the wisdom that the God metaphor represents to fill enough hearts to carry the day. That and the love that goes with the metaphor to hold us all together."

"Okay, I'm in. I'll put in a prayer card on Sunday."

"And so will I."

"Dottie, what are you doing on the line? I thought you agreed to work on your support system."

"That's what I'm doing. And I have an idea. Each of us should make two copies of our prayers and give one directly to Pastor Allen. That way if Mandy arranges for our prayer cards to be intercepted, Pastor will still have them."

"Pretty sneaky. Alice, do we want to start this whole campaign being sneaky?"

"Mandy already has."

"And I love her too much to let her get away with it."

9 PRAYERS OF THE PEOPLE

O come, O come Emmanuel and ransom captive Israel

Dottie couldn't figure out what she was going to wear. She stared at her closet full of woolen skirts and no-nonsense, white cotton, button-up blouses on their hangers, and the warm cardigan sweaters folded neatly on the shelf. It had taken her a whole day to move them in here from Glenda's room – ironic how quickly she stopped thinking of it as her room, or their room, or just the bedroom. It had been a good thing to do when she was still numb. It had filled her first day with mindless activity.

She hadn't planned to do it. That first night when they got home, she had actually gone to the bedroom, but when Glenda tried to hold her, it had been too close, too soon. She had pulled away and gone off to sleep in the guest room. Next morning when she woke up with no bathrobe or clean underwear close to hand, she had gone to get a few things, and then kept shuttling back and forth until all her clothes were in the closet, all her unmentionables were in the dresser, all her toiletries were in the bathroom. Not that she'd worn anything but pajamas and bathrobe for the last week plus.

Dottie had skipped breakfast and lunch. Around 5:00,

Glenda insisted that she have something. Dottie disinterestedly nibbled a little toast, sipped a little tea. It wasn't that she wanted not to eat, she just couldn't muster any enthusiasm for eating, for anything, but once Glenda got her seated at the table, Dottie thought, "Why not?" and went ahead and spooned down a little soup.

After dinner Glenda suggested that Dottie take a shower. *Funny*, Dottie thought, *I'm having trouble getting excited about that, too.* She had heard of rape victims who obsessively showered and showered and showered and were never able to wash away the feel of their attackers. She was never in that place and wondered why. Because she wasn't awake when they were lying on her? Because they never took all her clothes off and got their cooties all over her? Because even in the hospital, even when she got home, she was still in a bit of roofie haze, and it suppressed her feelings during the crisis phase when she should have been obsessing? Are there phases when things 'should' happen? Or was it because she felt them inside, not outside? *I know I can't wash them out of there, so I'm trying to suppress the feeling so I don't try and rip my uterus right out of my body.*

So here she was ten days later. She had promised Alice to support all of them officially coming out at church tomorrow. She couldn't go to church in her heart pajamas and flannel bathrobe (she hadn't worn the fuzzy one since…then), but she hated all her clothes. She hated her Berkshires uniform, the one the men had taunted her about. She hated it in the same way she hated the word 'lesbian.' They had spoiled both the word and the clothes for her. She hoped not forever – at least not the word. *Now that I'm out, and going to try to be more out, I need to own that word, wear it proudly as a badge of honor. But it's just a label. Why do we have to label things?*

I've got *to find something to wear. What else do I have?* Her summer dresses. Maybe. They keep the church pretty warm this time of year. Maybe the jeans and flannel shirt she used for working around the house. Where did she read that it's all about the way you want to come before your God? Something about some people promise their God to make an offering of their best self, and they symbolize that by coming to church in their best clothes. Others promise their God to bring what they are, flawed and broken, their everyday self, and they symbolize that by coming in their everyday clothes. But jeans and flannel weren't her everyday clothes. That was what Glenda wore every day. *And Glenda looks a hell of a lot better in jeans than I do.*

O my God! Jeans and flannel are what ... they *were wearing. Is that why I can't share a room with Glenda?*

She suddenly made up her mind. She threw on the jeans with a blouse and a cardigan – a little of each world, neither fish nor fowl, she could stand that for the time it would take to do what she had to do – and grabbed her purse and keys. "Glenda, I'm going out for a while." She headed for the garage. Now where to go? She still had that fear of people she'd admitted to Alice. Head for one of those little boutiques in Lenox? She wouldn't meet too many people there. On the other hand, the people she *did* meet would know her, would be waiting on her, fawning over her, worried about her, getting in her face, asking how she was. Plus, it was too close to...*there.*

No, this was a case of more is less. She'd go to the Lee Outlet Center and lose herself in the Christmas crowd. She'd be totally alone. No one would even recognize her if she was lucky. None of the news coverage had her name or her face. She could go into one of the big stores, get what she needed, get in an impersonal checkout queue, be rung out by a harried and overworked seasonal employee who wouldn't even have the time to look up at her, and get home before she lost her nerve.

Besides, all those Lenox boutiques mostly carried the items for the Berkshire uniform, and that was the look she was trying to ditch.

* * *

Glenda couldn't keep her mind on getting ready for church. She was getting worried about the B&B. She hadn't been there in ten days. Not since…not since That Night. Except once. To talk to Dave and tell him why she'd be otherwise occupied. She had come out to him. He hadn't been surprised. He said he knew Glenda and Dottie were important to each other, and of course he knew about the assault. It was all over the papers for three days. Even made the evening news on the Albany stations.

Dave was being an angel. Not in the sense of a well be-haved baby, and not in the sense of the terrifying avatar of the Divine that so often presaged bad news in the Bible, but in the sense of a Godsend. Somehow he was finding time to both take up the slack of running the Ferguson and keep tabs on Glenda and, through her, Dottie.

The two housekeepers, who had always been worth their weight in gold, were stepping up even more. Dave said that Maria was showing a lot of initiative and great business sense. She was helping with the books and the ordering. Her English might be limited but numbers are international. Juanita was cheerfully taking on the house-keeping that Maria was neglecting to help in the office, plus doing breakfast for the guests.

However, this was the off season. There weren't many beds to make, or many breakfasts to cook, or a lot of food to order. Glenda was glad to know that day-to-day could get along without her, but there was a lot more to the off season than day-to-day. There were repairs, improvements, long-range plans. She couldn't stay away forever.

She was also worried about herself. She hadn't been eating. How could she eat at a time like this? By now, she should be up at least ten pounds. Instead, she was down four from where she was at the end of the season, and eight from where she had been after Dottie's Thanksgiving feast.

Thanksgiving. What a time she and Dottie had had. She ached to have that Dottie back. Their whole Advent had been interrupted. She was used to thinking of her life in two seasons, Busy Season and Off Season, but now that she was missing it, she realized that Christmas Season was the third season of her life. They hadn't watched a Christmas movie since *Love, Actually*… What a good day that had been. What love they had shared. She couldn't remember if she cried more when Jamie and Aurelia got together or when Sarah and Karl didn't, but she knew she cried a lot more when Dottie moved into the guest room, and in a whole different way. From the bottom of her heart, not just the top layer.

She hadn't cried since. People thought Glenda was cold. She wondered if Dottie thought she was cold. She wasn't emotional. She wasn't moping around crying all the time. She seemed unaffected.

That was not the truth. The truth was she had cried all night that first night after she brought Dottie home from the hospital, after Dottie told her about all that had happened, and about all the blanks when she couldn't remember what happened but what the evidence said must have occurred. Glenda cried. She cried it all out. Now she could be strong for Dottie. She could be Dottie's rock, Dottie's anchor. Dottie could see that, couldn't she? Dottie knew how much Glenda loved her, didn't she?

Dottie was glad she'd laid out one of her new outfits last night. At least she didn't have to make that decision this morning. It's so much easier to choose clothes when you're not confronted with having to put them on immediately, and so much easier to get dressed when you've already decided what to wear. So Dottie was dressed. She just wasn't quite ready to go. Not inside.

Going out last night helped, Dottie thought. She was with people; some of them were even male, and she didn't melt. But they were people she didn't know. There was no one at the mall who she loved, no one who loved her, no one who knew who and what she was and hated her for it. No one who knew what she'd been through and hated or feared or felt sorry for her because of it. Everyone she would see this morning would be in at least one of those categories, feeling at least one of those feelings.

Her gut ached, even as her brain said, 'You can't control what others think and feel. All you can control is how you choose to react.' She stood in front of the full-length mirror. She looked herself in the eye and said that again. She said it out loud. Then she said it like she meant it.

"You can't control what others think and feel. All you can control is how you choose to react." *I look damn good in this new outfit, and I chose it. I'm a powerful woman, a force to be reckoned with. Look out, World, here I come.* And the body blows in her gut got worse than ever. She took a deep breath, threw her shoulders back, stuck out her chin, picked up her new coat and purse just as she heard Glenda calling her name. *Shut up, gut, I'm leading with my head.* It's time to be strong. Fake it 'til you make it.

"Dottie, time to get the car warmed up. Are you coming? Do you still feel up to this?" Glenda turned when she heard Dottie walk into the kitchen, and froze. She felt like a cliché as her jaw dropped and her eyes grew wide.

Dottie was wearing a tailored pant suit in Navy blue wool serge, a bright red silk blouse, and smart Navy pumps with a stylishly sensible one-and-a-half inch heel. "I'm ready." Dottie shrugged into her black boiled wool coat. "Bring it on. I'll drive."

Glenda had thought she was ready. Now she wasn't so sure. *I'm certainly not as ready as Dottie seems to be.*

One: God be with you
Many: And also with you
May the peace of Christ dwell in our hears
Christ is our peace, our light, and our hope
Let us pray.

"O God, to whom every thought is known, every heart is open, and every soul is laid bare, we know that these prayers are in your mind even before they are on our lips, but still we make bold to bring them before you.

"We give thanksgiving for the lives of those who have died: George Harris, Bob Michaels, and the mother of a friend at work, and we ask your healing grace on all those who mourn.

"With Jen we give thanks for Belle's tenth birthday. With Mandy we give thanks for the solid Christian faith of this church. With Alice, we offer prayers of concern for her son Trevor, going to school in North Carolina and threatened with having to change his dorm and his bathroom if he is outed as transgender to his school."

(Audible gasp.)

"With Glenda (louder gasp from Mandy's usual pew) we offer prayers of healing for Dottie after the trauma she has suffered. With Dottie…"

"What are you doing? We agreed… !"

"Sit down Mandy! With Dottie we give thanks for the guidance and friendship of Alice, whose own experience with healing from assault has made her a great comfort and guide, whose connection with the LGBT community has been a source of strength and courage, and thanks for the love and support of her partner Glenda."

10 NOTHING BUT REPEATS

Bells will be ringing the sad, sad news
O what a Christmas to have the blues

I'm down. Way down. Maybe hitting bottom, but I'm too low even to hold on to that hope. I feel like this could go on forever, just getting lower and lower and lower…

Mary came by earlier. All the docents stepped up to cover my hours until I can get back. She actually didn't say that. She was great. She didn't imply there was a time limit or a schedule. She just said everyone sends their love and they were covering my hours.

Then she hugged me. She hugged me in a way I haven't been hugged since…that night at the hospital. Glenda has been great, but you can tell she's worried. She handles me gently like she's afraid I'll break. And I thought I might. But Mary held me in a powerful embrace and I didn't break. If I weren't in such a bad place, if it weren't for Glenda and Doug, I think that hug might have led to a different kind of embrace. I'm so vulnerable right now, I was really tempted. Really tempted, and I think Mary would have gone for it. I think right now she'd do any-thing if she thought it would help me, but we both know it wouldn't. I kissed her on the cheek, and she kissed me on the cheek. Then I tried to kiss her for real and she let go and stepped away. That's when she said it: that we both know that it wouldn't help, it would just make it worse.

I don't know how Mary got away from Doug and the boys. I guess Christmas Eve isn't a big deal at their house. They're not church goers, and they don't let the boys open presents early. I remember when I was a kid we didn't even set up the tree and put out the presents until Christmas Eve, and then we left the tree up with the open presents under it for the Twelve Days of Christmas. Nowadays we all set up our trees in November, and on Christmas morning we tear into our presents and the whole season is over and past by noon and the town Christmas Tree pickup happens before New Year's Eve.

I guess that's part of what's getting me down. I really thought if I could catch the Christmas spirit it would help me out in moving forward, but instead I'm already feeling the letdown of Christmas being over too soon. Some of the neighbors won't even turn on their lights tomorrow night. I want Christmas to last. I even went to the post office and bought Christmas Forever stamps! I want my money back, and I know I'm going to feel worse tomorrow when it actually happens.

After we got past our hug and what almost happened, Mary and I talked for an hour. She kept reminding me of what Alice had said about having to go through the same steps over and over, and in my head I know that, but this hits in my gut. It's like blows to the body, except they come from the inside and there's no way to block them. They just keep coming and coming and it feels like they're never going to stop. It feels like I haven't gone through any steps at all.

Mary tells me I was doing better a few days ago. She said I was starting to be strong, to take an interest in things. If she says so. Right now I can't remember anything but this depression.

Glenda just brought me a nice cup of tea. With a scone.

One of her famous scones that she serves at the B&B on Friday and Saturday afternoon.

"Dottie, you know I love you."

I just nodded.

"And I know we can't force this, we can't hurry it. It takes time, and no one can predict how long it will take you."

I nodded again.

"But we're a couple. We're in this together. They say that when one person in a couple has cancer, they both have cancer, it's just in the body of one of them. This is just like that. We were violated by what they did to your body and we have to fight it. Together. I just wish there was more I could do for you."

I do, too. If we could catch the men who did this, if I could face them, if I could make them tell their story, if I could find out what *really* happened, what they did to me, it might help start the healing, but we're not getting anywhere. The blood tests came back positive for rohypnol and negative for STDs. And I'm not pregnant – although I'm not sure why they spent the money on that one.

But the justice system has abandoned me. With no memory except fancy boots, a ten-gallon hat, and a big belt buckle – none of which I can describe – the police have decided not to spend the money to process my rape kit. Even though the positive test for roofies pretty much makes rape a slam dunk.

Why does everyone say that? Why do I say that? I hate sports metaphors. I hate sports. That's why those guys looked so out of place in the café. They belonged in a sports bar.

Susan, bless her heart, fought tooth and nail for me. She came over in person yesterday to give me that news herself. On top of worrying about the coming out backlash, the future of the church, and the pre-Christmas dread of the post-Christmas letdown, Susan's news took the last wind out of my sails and left me adrift. Another sports metaphor, but at least it's a seagoing sport. Maybe the sea will soothe me.

Then add the unfulfilled longing for Mary. Yes, I admit it. While in my head I know it won't help, that's the same head that is totally failing to make me feel better about repeating stages. The gut that is taking the body blows wants to hold on to Mary and never let go until I've touched and been touched everywhere and in every way.

All the fears are right there, and now I've got the new one: that I'll never get justice. And the fear of never finding out what happened just became more real. If the case isn't solved, I won't get closure, justification and an end to imagining how bad it might have been – imaginings that are worse than the physical evidence says it could ever have been, worse than it could have been because I'm still alive. In most of my dreams I don't even survive. Today I'm not sure that I have.

Who is going to abandon me next? Mary? – she'll get tired of covering for me. Susan? – she already has another rape case. Sheri? – she already has two more; her area is bigger than Susan's. Alice? – she wants support in the fight to make Third Methodist a reconciling congregation, and I don't think I have the energy or the spirit for that. Glenda? – she'll get tired of waiting for me to come back to bed. My head understands women who don't want to be with their man after they've been raped, but it doesn't understand why my gut won't let Glenda touch me, especially when it wanted – wants – so badly for Mary to touch me. Forbidden fruit v. wanting me too much? Punishing Glenda for not stopping them? Punishing Mary for loving Doug more than me? Punishing myself for being raped?

Punishing myself. Not letting myself have the love that would do me good, and pushing away my best friend by trying to force a relationship that will only hurt me. I am so fucked up.

Punishing myself. That's the big fear: that the next person who will abandon me is Dottie. I'm afraid that I'll just give up and stop trying. Maybe stop living. Maybe not survive. It would end the pain. But as much as my gut wants that, I think my head would stop me. It knows it will get better.

11 ACTS OF RECONCILIATION

I pulled in [from] Nazareth, was feelin' 'bout half past dead
I just need a place where I can lay my head
Hey, Mister, can you tell me where a man might find a bed?

I'm going to speak this evening on the Nativity. Not on the Nativity story – those of you who were with us at 5:30 for the family service saw the young people act out the story far more eloquently than my meagre skills of description or elaboration could ever hope to do.

An old teacher of mine taught me to make the literal into something symbolic and the symbolic into something literal. Joseph Campbell says that everything is a symbol. He is very specific about the symbolism in the Bible – some of it, anyway. He picks and chooses. He expounds on the symbolism of some of the stories, but mostly he talks about the broad elements of the whole Bible narrative. What do crucifixion and resurrection stand for? What is the symbolism of Mary? Of the Virgin birth? The Garden? The Fall? The Exodus?

I would like to see Campbell speak to every element. I would like to see Campbell go through the Bible story by story, passage by passage, verse by verse and tell us what the symbolism is and how it relates to the broad-brush symbolism he has shown us. As far as I can tell from my reading, he never did that, and it's too late for him to do it now. So when I come upon a passage, I have to try and ferret out the symbolism on my own.

When my atheist niece brought me a terra cotta Nativity from Palermo last summer, it led me to ponder: what symbolism does this knick-knack contain that an atheist would be able to relate to? The answer turned out to be pretty simple: simple to find but hard to fathom. The Nativity is the symbol for the entry of the divine into the temporal realm. The Birth of Jesus symbolizes the moment when a human being becomes aware of the divinity inherent in themselves and in each human being they encounter. The moment when God is born in human form.

And that birth is a Virgin birth. Only one person is involved, one person in relationship to their divinity, to their god.

Although we use the Nativity as a symbol for the Divine entering Jesus and by extension each of us, I think it is more likely that Jesus had what Alan Watts would call his Moment of Cosmic Consciousness in the wilderness during the 40 days. The busyness of human interaction can keep the Devil at bay. While the Devil may tempt us in the form of other people, it is only when we are in solitude, where we can confront and defeat the evil inside ourselves and do it alone, that we are able to unlock our full divinity.

Does that mean that only some of us have divinity inside? No, not at all. Some of us do a better job of unlocking it. Some of us fail miserably. That is why the Buddhists and the Hindi find it optimistic to believe in two, three, or seventy times seven tries at it.

But just because it is untapped doesn't mean the spark isn't there. This is where we make the symbolic into the literal. Look to your left. That person has divinity inside them. Look to your right. That person has a divine spark. Now tap the shoulder of the person in in front of you. When they turn around, say, 'Namasté. I honor the divine spark within you.'

Who was the neighbor of the man who fell among thieves on the road to Jericho? The Samaritan. The most unlikely person. The person, however, who recognized his own spark of divinity in this man who had been robbed, stripped, and beaten. He knew who his neighbor was.

Now let's get down to brass tacks. We have here with us tonight people who have suffered, who are our neighbors, who we should reach out to. As a result of a horrific sexual assault – and I use that phrase not to avoid the more shocking 'rape' but to highlight that this is an extreme form of the misuse, subjugation, inequality, and oppression that some minimize under the rubric 'sexual politics' – as a result of this sexual assault, this congregation became aware of certain truths about the gender identities of some of our members. Some among us see that as a reason to drive them from our doors. They take their cue from the Methodist *Book of Discipline* which finds homosexuality to be incompatible with Christian teaching. Certain people want to force their neighbors out, and if they can't do that, freeze them out.

When they tried to recruit me to their project, I didn't say 'no.' That was my failing. I stand here now to apologize to Glenda, Dottie, Alice, and anyone else who is LGBT or involved with someone who is – in or out. I cannot rationalize what I did, I can only try to make it right, and the first step is to tell you all, 'No.' No, I will not work with you to force anyone out of the Church. Jesus never turned anyone away from his table and neither will I. Not anymore.

Now I hear what you're thinking. What about Leviticus 18:22? 'Thou shalt not lie with mankind as with womankind: it is an abomination.' And I answer, what about Leviticus 11:10? 'And all that have not fins and scales in the seas, and in the rivers, of all that move in the waters, and of any living thing which is in the waters, they shall be an abomination unto you.' When was the last time you had a lobster roll, or clam chowder, or bay scallops, or raw oysters? Now, I'm not talking about Manhattan clam chowder. That *is* an abomination.

And you answer, yes, but in Acts 11:5 Peter had a vision that anything God had made was not unclean. That's why we can tuck into a baked lobster stuffed with crabmeat, or a BLT for that matter.

Well, I see your vision – pun intended – and raise you an actual physical encounter. In Acts 8, as you recall, Philip is taken bodily by the Spirit to the side of the road where a eunuch is passing by in a chariot, reading scripture. Now if a homosexual is unclean, how much more unclean must a eunuch be? Because a gay person is just the way God made them, but a eunuch becomes a eunuch by the hand of man, in violation of God's intent for the person. Deuteronomy 23:1 tells us, 'He that is wounded in the stones, or hath his privy member cut off, shall not enter into the congregation of the LORD.' Yet at the end of the story, the eunuch says, 'See, here is water; what doth hinder me to be baptized?' And Philip is shown, by the Spirit and by the divine spark in the eunuch, that, if it is not possible that any food made by God is unclean, how much less is it possible that a person made by God can be unclean? Philip answers, 'If thou believest with all thine heart, thou mayest.' And as soon as Philip has done God's work by baptizing the eunuch, the Spirit returns him to Azotus. It was if nothing had happened. But everything had changed.

As you prepare to celebrate Christmas, as we prepare to invite one another to the communion table, think on this: Mary was an unwed mother, but she was not unclean. Joseph was a lecherous old man, but he was not unclean. The shepherds lived in the fields with the sheep, but they were not unclean. The Magi were heathens from a pagan land and probably not circumcised, but they were not unclean. And Jesus was born among the donkey dung and slept on top of a cow's supper, but He most assuredly was not unclean.

Let it be so.

* * *

As Pastor Allen spoke, Mandy sat with her arms folded across her chest and her legs pressed together. When others were looking left and right, she didn't move, and when she was tapped on the shoulder, she didn't turn around. She just pursed her lips into a tighter line.

But those who sat near her thought they saw the least glimmer of a tear in the corner of her eye. Whether it was for her church, or for the Pastor, or for herself, no one could guess. Even Mandy didn't know. But part of her, a part she was afraid of, a part she was trying to ignore, thought that maybe, just maybe, it was for Dottie.

12 DICK

Met my old lover at the grocery store
The snow was falling. Christmas Eve.

It's starting to snow. I'm pulling into my neighborhood just as the flakes begin to stick to the pavement. Just like they were that Thursday night three weeks ago. It's pulling me right back to that night. It's like I just did it all over again.

George made us do it. It was all his idea.

Not that I'm trying to evade responsibility. I did it. I went along. Not just for the ride. I took my turn with her.

It was also George's idea to keep her panties. He took that fancy knife off his belt and cut them into four pieces. He gave Harry the big piece that covered her fat ass.

He gave Tom and me each a side piece, from over the hips. George kept the crotch for himself. George was the one who pulled up her skirt and half pulled/half ripped her panties off over her wool knee socks, knocking off her lesbo sandals. He said they smelled real good, like hot tuna, but he didn't let any of the rest of us confirm that. Just stuffed them in the back pocket of his jeans. It wasn't until later that he divvied them up.

Getting her to the 4X4 wasn't easy. People were giving

us the hairy eye. George kept saying, "She's not feeling well" and "She can't handle her liquor." Somehow he got away with it, even though people could see she'd only been drinking coffee. Hell, the waiter knew he hadn't brought her anything but coffee. Everyone had seen that she didn't even want to dance with George, she surely didn't want to leave with him. I think the waiter knew what was going on and wanted to go with us, and everyone else was afraid to speak up. George got them to play their parts just like Tom, Harry and me played ours.

George made us all wear his hat while we were taking our turns. That way, he said, if she woke up enough to see us, all our faces would be confused with one hat, and it would mix her all up. I think he just wanted to feel like it was him fucking her all four times. Five – he *did* fuck her twice. None of the rest of us could get it up a second time. Hell, I think Harry had trouble getting it up the first time.

They say rape isn't about sex, it's about power. I always thought that missed the point. All sex is about power – just different kinds of power. I found out about more kinds of power when George took over. I feel like it wasn't four of us raping that lady. It was George raping four of us: that lady, Tom, Harry, and me. He bent us to his will and made us have sex with him. He was just using that lady's body for all the rapes.

I haven't seen Harry or Tom all month. Or George, for that matter. Maybe he went back out West. The rest of us are just lying low.

I didn't expect to see her at that church. I went far out of town to try and hide. But I couldn't hide from God, or from myself. To hear her name spoken from the pulpit! Dottie – I never knew her name. And to hear myself condemned for my actions. I wonder if the Preacher even imagined that one of us was there.

I can't imagine what Dottie is going through. I still can't believe what George got us to do. It still feels like I was another victim, but Dottie is the real victim. This snow is just rubber-banding me back, and it was only my will that was violated. Her will was totally taken away, and her body violated – repeatedly. On top of it all I guess she doesn't even remember what happened, only what it felt like to wake up and realize something was wrong.

That Preacher was speaking directly to me tonight. Dottie is my neighbor. I let George's crass remarks and taunts about her clothes and insinuations about her sexual orientation blind me to that. He put a veil over her divine spark. Boy, did I let the Devil tempt me, and the fact that he took the form of a friend was part of how he clouded my eyes. Only when I'm alone do I wrestle with what went on that night. Do I have any divine spark left in me after what I've done? How many times will I have to be reincarnated to live this one down?

I'm going to have to turn myself in. I'll go to my parents' for Christmas dinner tomorrow. I'll let them have one more holiday with their perfect son. Monday I'll get Phil to go down to the station with me. I guess it makes sense to have my lawyer, even though I plan to basically screw myself to the wall. Phil will help to make sure the screws are legally binding. Of course, he'll try to talk me out of it, or get me to turn state's evidence, or go for a plea bargain. I need to toughen my resolve before I even talk to him. I'm not turning in Tom and Harry – they'll have to decide in their own consciences what to do. As far as I'm concerned, they were victims just like me.

I want to remember to take my piece of the panties. That should make them sit up and pay attention. I'm not just another wierdo trying to become famous by a false confession.

I don't know what to do about George. I think he was more at fault than Tom and Harry. I can hear what George would say. That I can't change anything, that I can't undo what was done, and I'm just going to hurt a lot more people if the truth comes out. That's a tough one to answer. How can I do this to my folks? and maybe Tom's, Harry's, and George's families, too. But it's only justice. It's only the truth. The hurt was done to them as surely as to Dottie and the people who love her on that Thursday. It's just that they're still asleep. They haven't discovered yet how they have been violated. Keeping them in the dark won't change the violation, just delay the recovery.

And Dottie. She deserves to know. She deserves to hear the whole story. It may not make her whole, but without it she won't have a chance.

But even though I blame George, if I finger him it's like I'm trying to displace some of my blame. I can't do that. No Tom or Harry, then no George. George, wherever you are, you're safe for now.

Funny, I feel a connection to Dottie that she will never feel with me. Sex is a connection, even when it's not about sex, even when it's a violation. In a way she's one of my lovers – and I haven't had enough to forget any of them.

13 CHRISTMAS

Love came down at Christmas, Love all holy, Love divine
Love came down at Christmas, Stars and angels gave the sign

Glenda woke up first. At least she thought she did. She couldn't be sure. Dottie wasn't making a sound from the guest room where she had moved when they got home from the hospital. Glenda winced at the irony. For years they had maintained the fiction of separate bedrooms. Now that everyone knew it had been a fiction, it was true again.

Glenda slipped a small package out of her dresser drawer and into the pocket of her bathrobe – the same fluffy bathrobe she wore to Thanksgiving dinner. She wondered what Dottie's reaction would be when she found out Glenda was wearing the same frilly nothings under it, too. Maybe too obvious, but what she had planned was all or nothing. There was no turning back.

She padded down the hall in her bear feet. She loved her bear-paw slippers that Dottie had given her, let's see, three years ago today. They were holding up remarkably well. Dottie always did go for quality. Glenda turned up the heat, turned on the lights on the Christmas tree, added the small gift to the pile, and went into the kitchen to start the coffee. She should have gone to the Berkshire Mountain Bakery for something for breakfast. Chocolate bread would have been perfect. Neither one of them had been eating well since Dottie's rape. She would be worrying about not putting the weight back on, she was actually losing more, if she weren't so worried about everything else. They couldn't go on like this, they needed their strength. Pastor Allen had issued the challenge to Mandy & Co. Ltd. (at least she hoped they were limited to the ones she knew about) and the coming fight was going to be nothing less than a struggle for the future soul of Third Methodist. She hoped that what she had planned for this morning wouldn't start another fight. Food was still not on her mind.

Dottie heard Glenda moving around. Glenda was trying to be quiet. If Dottie had been sleeping, she certainly would have slept through it. So Glenda must be up to something. She'd give her space, even though she ached for her partner, her friend, her lover. At least the ache was progress. After Pastor Allen's sermon, Dottie, Glenda, Alice and Pastor had hugged one another. Who knew if it was joy, relief, or terror? But Dottie had hugged Glenda the hardest and the longest. The only reason she was still in the guest room was she didn't know whether Glenda was ready to take her back yet, didn't know how to ask. After all their years together, this had turned them into strangers, and she didn't know how to bridge the gulf that had opened up. A magnitude eight earthquake is nothing compared to a gang rape.

Okay, she could smell the coffee brewing. Glenda must have known that would wake Dottie up, so whatever Glenda was up to, whatever she wanted to accomplish while she had the house to herself, she must have gotten done. Dottie threw her bathrobe on over her flannel pajamas and headed for the bathroom. After throwing some water on her face and doing a quick Listerine rinse, she paused, took off her bathrobe, took off her pajamas, and put her bathrobe back on. She didn't think Glenda would ever know, that they would go there today, but it gave her hope just to make the gesture, even if it was only to herself. She headed for the kitchen.

Glenda intercepted Dottie in the living room. The tree lights cast an intimate glow in the early morning December half light, and there was Dottie's coffee on the table, in her favorite mug and fixed, Dottie was sure, just way she liked it. "Merry Christmas!" Glenda got up and opened her arms wide.

"Merry Christmas." Dottie gave her a hug. Not as long and as hopeful as at Church last night. The excitement of the sermon had had time to fade. Dottie had had time to think about the chasm they had to cross, and the more she thought, the wider it seemed to gape. They did give each other a peck on the cheek. Perfunctory, but the first kiss they had had since the hospital.

With few words, they fell into their Christmas routine. They started with the stockings. Some candy, apples and oranges, a few office essentials wrapped to look more Christmassy than they really were. Two new pairs of socks for Dottie; working as a docent meant a lot of time on her feet and that was hard on her hosiery.

There weren't many presents under the tree. There never were – Dottie and Glenda both preferred to spend their money on shares of livestock with Heifer International or buckets of nails with Habitat for Humanity – but somehow the usual small pile looked more forlorn and overlooked this year.

Everything looks forlorn this year, Dottie thought.

I didn't do enough, I'm not doing enough, I never do enough, thought Glenda, *but maybe that one extra gift will do it.*

It didn't take long to get through the pile, even taking turns, even being careful not to incur bad luck by cutting ribbons, even removing the paper carefully so it could be reused, even taking the time to write down each gift and it's giver in the new memo books using the new pens, both of which were traditional stocking stuffers. So it didn't take Dottie long to find the small box that hadn't been there last night.

"What's this?"

"Open it."

A small diamond mounted on a thin band of gold winked up at Dottie.

"Okay, I'll ask again. What is it?"

"It's my grandmother's engagement ring. She thought someday some nice boy would put it on my finger and ask me to marry him. Now I'd like to put it on some nice girl's finger. Dottie, will you marry me? Will you stand up before God and our friends – and enemies – and declare we belong to each other forever? I know what you're going to say. We have a lot of problems, a lot of pressures, a lot of reasons not to get married, but I've been thinking about it, and I think that the things that look like reasons not to get married are really the best reasons *to* get married. Marriage is two people saying to each other, 'You and my love for you are more important to me than anything the world can throw at us, and I hereby commit to figuring out how to *not* let these problems break us up.' Dottie, I'm saying that to you. Will you say that to me?"

Dottie gave a big, wracking sob and ran from the room. *Damn* Glenda thought. *Now I've done it. She's probably in her room crying her eyes out and cursing me.* Or packing. She could hear drawers being pulled open and slammed shut. *I should go to her and apologize.* Glenda started to get up. *No, I should let her have her space.* She sat back down. *But if I just sit here, she'll think I didn't really mean it.* She started to get up. *Don't push.* She sat back down. *But I love her, I have to be by her side.* Glenda had started to get up and had sat back down a dozen times at least in the space of a minute and a half, when Dottie came rushing, practically running, back into the living room and thrust a small jewelry box into Glenda's hands.

"What's this?"

"Open it."

Two thin gold bands lay side by side, nestled in the aging velvet lining.

"Okay, I'll ask again. What is it?"

"It's my parents' wedding rings. I'm sure we can find a jeweler that can make them work for us. Yes, I'll tell the world you are the most important thing to me and I won't let anything break us up. Glenda, will you marry me?"

"Dottie, I will never abandon you."

Glenda and Dottie soon discovered what their partner was wearing under their Thanksgiving bathrobe. After a Christmas Nap with a capital "N" they watched both *Miracle on 34th Street* **and** *White Christmas*. They have a lot of catching up to do on their Christmas movie list. But they do have the Twelve Days of Christmas to do it in. And a good supply of Christmas Forever stamps.

14 BOXING DAY

Monday, Monday, can't trust that day
Monday, Monday, sometimes it just works out that way

"Ms. Conklin, this is Officer Johnson."

"Who?"

"Dottie, it's Susan."

"Susan! How are you?"

"I'm down at the station and Sheri is on her way. Can you come down and join us?"

"Is something wrong?"

"No, I think we might have a break. A man who says he was one of your attackers just turned himself in."

"Who is he?"

"He gives his name as Richard Lee, and has ID that corroborates. He calls himself Dick. Does that ring any bells?"

"No, should it?"

"Probably not. He says he doesn't know you, except from seeing you around Lenox and winding up in your church on Christmas Eve. And, of course, the night of the attack. Plus he says he has something of yours."

"I'll be right down."

"Just give my name to the desk sergeant and show him

your driver's license. He'll be expecting you."

"May I help you?"

"I'm here to see Officer Susan Johnson? She said to show my ID. I'm...

"No reason to say it out loud in this public space. Just sign in here. Your visitor badge is number 12. Susan, I mean Officer Johnson, will meet you right inside those double doors."

"Dottie, how are doing?" Susan thought, *She looks good. Not great, but good. New clothes. Taking care of herself. But that hug – I felt her need to hold on just a little longer, to have just that extra bit of human reassurance. She's drawing out the one with Sheri even more.*

"It's so good to see you both. What's it been, two weeks?"

"At least that since I last checked in on you, and Susan says she hasn't had any contact with you for almost three weeks. You haven't checked in at the center."

"I had a couple of friends come out of the woodwork, one totally unexpected and very supportive. Alice really helped me get past the frozen phase – at least for now – and back out in the world. Of course, it's limited, and people keep telling me that backslides are unavoidable, but for now I'm making progress, and I'm sure you're keeping busy."

"Always too busy. In this job the only good news is no news, but we haven't had that for a while."

"And Susan. I thought this was going to take time, and they weren't going to process the rape kit. What is this big break?"

"It almost sounds like we have Alice to thank. To listen to the suspect, if you hadn't gotten out in time to go to church for Christmas Eve Saturday, it might not have had so much impact on him. As it was, seeing you again in combination with the sermon by your preacher – Pastor

Allen, is it? – made him decide he wouldn't be able to live with himself if he didn't turn himself in. That's what he did, first thing this morning."

"So what's the next step?"

"This is really uncharted territory. He not only turned himself in, he says he wants to plead guilty to the maximum charge. He doesn't want to plea bargain or turn State's evidence against the other three – he says it's up to them what they need to do – and he doesn't want to decrease the sentence. He brought a lawyer – he says so no one can claim he was coerced or things weren't on the up-and-up. So the Chief of Detectives and the DA aren't quite sure how carefully to proceed. They're not going to do a lineup because it looks like they won't need your eyewitness testimony, but before they let him hang himself, they want to check out his story. Part of that is letting you see him, and having you identify this."

"That looks like a piece of the panties I was wearing that day. I guess. With the roofies I don't really remember, but those are the only ones that I'm missing."

"Do we have your permission to do a DNA check on them and compare it to the samples we took in the hospital? Yours and your attackers?"

"Yes, of course. Do I have to sign something?"

"It's in the observation room. We have Mr. Lee in the interrogation room, right on the other side of the one-way glass there. The other thing we want to know is if he looks familiar."

"No, and yes. One of a score of men that drink in Lenox in jeans and flannel. Not seared into my brain. Not the guy in the boots and hat – him I think I would remember after he tried to dance with me – but yeah, he could be one of them. He fits the type."

"I'm going to go in and record his confession. Would you like to stay?"

"Yes, thank you."

Sheri interrupted. "He might say some things in the

conference room that could be hard to hear. I know you want to know the truth, but I'm sure Susan will let you read the transcript later."

"No, I want to hear him say it. I want to watch his face. Susan, can Sheri stay with me?"

"I think that would be a good idea."

"We are here recording the confession of Richard Lee in the case of the alleged sexual assault of Dorothea Conklin. Present are officer Susan Johnson, Detective Sergeant Bill Wilson, Mr. Lee, and his lawyer, Attorney Howe.

"Please state your name for the record."

"Richard Henry Lee. Yes, named after the Revolutionary War general. You can call me Dick."

"Mr. Lee, are you making this confession of your own accord, without coercion or duress?"

"Yes."

"Then please tell your story in your own words."

I don't really know why we did it. We've never done anything like that before. Hell, we aren't even that close of friends. I guess now we never will be. Although we'll always have one thing in common.

No, I won't name names. This is on me, they have to live with their own consciences. I'll just call the others Tom, Harry, and George. That's right, as in this could have been any Tom, Dick, or Harry. Anyone could fall into this if they let go of their better judgement, and let George do it and just go along. That's what we did.

But I get ahead of myself.

It all started with the pill. George found out about someone who is dealing roofies, yes, rohypnol. I'd like to find out who he is. No, come to think of it, he never did say for sure that it was a man. I'd still like to get that sucker. No, I'm not blaming them, but it's like a loaded gun. We pulled the trigger and we didn't have to and I live with that, but the dealer left the loaded gun lying around. We'd talked about it a few times before. It's a loaded situation. It was like watching a rape trial on LA Law. You're simultaneously repulsed by the violence and inhumanness – is that a word? – and excited by the sexual nature of the crime – especially because you know it wasn't a real person, it was just a TV character, just an actress reading her lines about something she hadn't really experienced, not even as an actress because the crime was all off camera.

So we're sitting around talking about the fact that there are roofies on the street, and what we would like to do, and what we would do if we had a woman completely in our power. All purely hypothetical, you know – a hypothetical woman, not a real, flesh-and-blood person. Except the next thing you know George has bought one. Only one. That's what he said. This isn't going to become a thing, he says, it's just research. A one-time experiment to see if the stuff really works and we really follow through.

It's like in *The Fan Club* where the guys sit around the bar watching the talk show. The hot new Hollywood starlet, she wants to ramp up the hotness of her image, she starts telling the show host how there are no real men left, no men who would just take her and be the man and have their way with her. They convince themselves that they could be that guy, so when she comes to town, they've all talked so big that none of them can back out, they've talked themselves into abduction and rape.

Well, we talked ourselves into believing an experiment was justified in the name of science. Or some such shit. Sorry, I guess you can edit that out. I didn't really believe it, I was just talking a good game, and the same was probably true of Tom and Harry. I don't think it was that way for George or he wouldn't have bought the pill. Anyway, once he did, we let our male egos overshadow our sense of right. Our egos and that part of us that reads about a rape investigation for the words 'partially nude body.' We were in.

It was George who targeted Big Butt, ah, I mean the

victim. She seemed an unlikely target, mostly middle-aged frumpy. At the time I thought she was just what we used to call in the Navy a target of opportunity. We had been drinking in *Get Lit* and checking out the women there, but for some reason George left *Get Lit* and headed for the café around the corner. Big Butt, that's what George called her when he saw her, was the only woman in there alone, so I thought that's why we went for her, but looking back, trying to replay events, I can almost convince myself that he saw her through the window, recognized her from somewhere, and picked that café with the intent of singling her out as the victim.

As soon as we got into the café, George started hitting on her. He kept calling her a lesbian, taunting her with the word. Kept calling her a 'lesbian bitch.' Funny, I just re-membered a meme I read that said, ' "Bitch" is a word we use to take away a woman's right to say "no" and "slut" is a word we use to take away her right to say "yes." ' I guess 'roofie' is a word we use to take away her right to say any-thing.

When we were talking about it in the abstract, I thought it was going to be about sex. I found out it was really about power, and I didn't like having that kind of power. I didn't like George having that kind of power. I didn't like giving up my power to say yes or no, giving it up to group momentum, giving it up to George.

As Dick told the story of the events of December first, he thought about how he would have heard that story himself not so long ago, about how he thought about that night right up until it actually happened. Fantasy had been the mainstay of his sex life for a long time, and rape fantasies held a prominent place. However, he had learned some-thing important about rape. While the fantasy may be about sex, the reality most assuredly is not.

I know that wasn't easy on Dottie, Sheri thought. *She had the deer-in-the-headlights look I know so well. She never took her eyes off the suspect. Like that first night, in the hospital. Another brand new trauma. I was sharing my attention between Dottie, the suspect, and Officer Johnson. Susan was looking grim. Probably pretty much the way I was looking. We've heard the story so many times, but usually we hear it from the victim's point of view. It was kind of surreal to hear a suspect admitting to all the details – usually they try to deny most of them. But – Dick? is that his name? – gave us details Dottie will probably never be able to remember.* "Are you okay?"

"I think so."

"Then can I have my arm back? You've had a death grip on it for the last twenty minutes."

"Oh, sorry, I've been in there with them. And back on the mountain."

"No, it's okay. I almost felt that way myself, and it wasn't me he was talking about."

"Still, I hope I didn't hurt you." *They're leading…*him *out. Good. I don't care if I never see him again.* "Susan is leaving."

"She's probably headed here. She'll join us in just a second." *And there's the doorknob rattling.*

"Is everything okay in here? How are you holding up, Dottie?"

"I'm ready to sit down, and I could really use some water – no ice. Tap is fine."

"Bill, could you bring me a couple of glasses of water, one with no ice? Anything for you, Sheri?"

"Coffee, black, two sugars."

"Got that, Bill? Thanks." *I'll just give her until the drinks get here to settle down. We can all stand a little silence, to absorb what we heard.* "Here we are."

"Thanks, that hit the spot." *It was so unreal. I think I was holding my breath half the time. That must be what it was like before television, back in the days of the great radio dramas. Just listening, it was like I was there. I was, and I wasn't. My body was there, I know, but I have no memory. So it was all make believe, a fiction, but I know it wasn't. Holding, drinking, an actual glass of water kind of brings me back to reality.* "At least now I won't have to make up what I don't know. Now I know."

"Yes, you do, but it might not change that much." Sheri spoke from experience – hers and others. "You'll likely still imagine all sorts of things that *could* have happened, and if you've been having nightmares, I suspect they will continue for some time. They will get less frequent, but they will never stop completely. It's one of the gifts Dick and his cronies have given you."

"I've talked to the Chief. We're going to get your evidence kit out of cold storage and process it after all. It's a long shot, but with Dick in custody – he's declining bail, by the way, says that's just part of his penance – we have a chance of tracking down his cronies. It's the pharmacist I'd like to get my hands on, though. Ever since he – I have to believe it's not one of us women – ever since he hit town rape has gone up 300%.

"And that rape counselor Sheri recommended. Did she contact you? You may not be ready, but one of the times she calls, you are probably going to say 'yes'."

"Yes, she did. Thanks."

"Have you thought about what you'll do if we catch Tom, Harry, or George? Are you going to want to face them in court? Are you going to want to testify?" Later Dottie couldn't remember if it was Sheri or Susan who asked that, but they were both thinking it.

"Of *course*!! I'm not going to let them get away with it! I want them off the street before they can hurt anyone else!"

"Don't say that too quickly. Have you thought about having to face them in court? That's always tough; for you it might make the rape even more real because right now you only have one face."

"Have you thought about testifying? I know you have to tell your story repeatedly to a lot of people, but that is in your control. Do you really want to relive the whole experience the way a good prosecutor will get you to tell it?"

"And then there's cross. Do you really want a defense attorney, an authority figure, an officer of the court, telling you it was your fault, you asked for it, you wanted it?"

"Please, stop, you're scaring me! You're tag-teaming me! It's like you don't want me to testify!"

"We do. We do want you to testify. That's why we want to give you time to think about all the reasons not to, all the scary parts, so that when the time comes, you're prepared, not taken by surprise by a whole bunch of new feelings a whole handful of new traumas. I'm sure Susan will back me up on this."

"Now I really don't know."

"We'll talk more about this. I'll call you next week, or sooner if anything happens. Call any time you need or want to, any time there's anything you need or want. You have the numbers? The center and my mobile?"

"Yes, right by the phone, and on speed dial on my Android."

"Do you want to give me that number?"

"No, not yet, but thank you."

"You keep going. Keep telling your story. The more it becomes part of you the less it can hurt you. The less you'll be a rape victim and the more you'll become a rape survivor, and then just a person who was raped."

"Never just a person?"

"No, that's not in the cards."

"Can I have a squad car take you home?"

"No, thank you, Glenda is down the block having a Dunkin' waiting for me."

"Really? She could have come over here. She could have been here."

"No, I wanted to do this myself. I want to tell her what I learned in my own way. I want – we both want – this to be about her and me, not her and me and them, for her to hear my story, not his."

"I guess that sounds sensible."

"But I'm awfully glad you were here, Sheri. I don't think I could have heard that alone, even with Susan just on the other side of the mirror."

"Well, I hope everything works out for you. Know I'm here – the whole center is here – for you." *That hug felt a little more relaxed, a little more friendly. A little less needy.*

15 CHECKING IN

Hello? Is it me you're looking for?

Damn. It feels so impersonal having to put someone in a tickler file so I don't forget to call. Susan says it's the new source in town. What does she call it? A pharmacist. I bet it won't be long before the papers pick up on that name and capitalize it. 'Authorities are actively seeking an unknown subject they refer to as The Pharmacist. Police believe he or she is responsible for a rash of sexual assaults which they attribute to a new source of rohypnol, also called "roofies" or "date-rape drug."' I'm not sure. Yeah, survivors on roofies are up, but I feel like we've seen an increase in those that don't involve drugs, too. Funny, isn't it. I'm so busy I don't have the time to run the numbers, to look at all the case files and categorize and count and check up on my impressions. I'm too busy to figure out why I'm so busy. I don't even have time to check in with my cases unless I put a reminder in my phone. Next.

"Dottie? Hi, it's Sheri."

"Hi, Sheri, what can I do for you?"

"That's my question. I'm just checking in to see if you need anything I can provide. How are you doing?"

"I'm kind of stuck. I'm functioning. I'm coping, but

what is it they say in those drug commercials? Coping seems to be all that I do."

That's what this stage is all about, but I can't say that to her. She's a person, not a victim, not a case, not someone who is going through a 'stage.' "Believe me, we've all been there."

"We?"

"We don't talk about it much, but most of us at the crisis center got into this work because rape has touched us or someone close to us — which is almost the same thing. When someone close is raped, it affects everyone around them."

"You know, Glenda said something like that on Christmas Eve. She said we'd both been raped, they just did it to my body." She had a faint memory from the E.R. that Sheri had talked about being pulled back to her past...

"She is very wise. I'm not sure I would have put it quite that way, but I've never had a partner who was raped."

"Glenda is great, but she has more space than I do. She can forget. She wasn't there; she can go to a place where she can put it out of her mind for a time."

"Does it bother you that she forgets?"

"No. I'm glad she can — that way one of us can cope with the rest of life — but I'm jealous of her ability to compartmentalize. My body won't let me forget."

"You're not dealing with life?"

"I'm trying to get out, but it's still hard. I don't feel safe. Sleeping is hard. The nightmares, the imagination. I still feel sticky down there. That's the one thing they left me that I felt when I was awake. For some reason, I flash back on that even more than the cold and the pain."

"What else?"

"Retail therapy. I started out with a few new outfits."

"I saw one when we were at the station. Looked nice. Susan thought so, too."

"But now I seem to be trying to totally redefine myself as 'not that person who got raped.'"

"That could be good or bad. You're not the same person as you were before the assault. You will have to work to define the new person. However, if you're trying to define yourself as someone else, someone who never was and never would be raped, that's denial. You'll have to go through some of it, but getting caught in it can be damaging."

"And expensive. It's a good thing I'm back at work."

"How is that going?"

"I have good days and bad days. I have trust issues. I have people issues. Some days I like the security of the crowds. Other days I remember that they took me right out of a crowded place. Of course I never drink anything at work. I don't know what someone might put in it. I keep small bottles of water in my locker. I take one out, break the seal, drink the whole thing, lock my locker and recycle the bottle."

"That may be your new reality."

"But it doesn't make sense. There are so many other ways I can be attacked, why focus on that one?"

"That will take time. For now what you have to do is whatever it takes for you to feel safe."

"I just feel so OCD."

"It's a perfectly normal reaction to your rape. You have had a trauma. In my opinion just about the worst trauma a human being can have. So severe that you're probably still experiencing new traumas, discovering new ways you have been traumatized, finding out more parts of your life that are always going to be different than they were. You're strong, you survived, you're moving forward. A little OCD is what any normal human being would feel after an inhuman experience."

"Yeah, I guess. My friends have helped a lot."

"Which brings me to my next question: How is your network?"

"Strong. Glenda is great. Did you know we're engaged? We're still taking it slow, but she's understanding and supportive. Mary, the friend I told you about at the hospital, is a rock, and I have a new ally. Alice, a woman from church who I had dismissed as one of 'those.' Turns out she is a rape survivor, and she also has a transgender son, which has made her an LGBT ally. She's really helping on both counts. She helped Glenda and I come out officially at church."

"I thought you outed yourself at the hospital?"

"I did, but that was accidental and left room for interpretation. This was planned and purposeful. We declared that we weren't going to sneak around anymore."

"How does that feel?"

"Scary. Good. Scary-good. It's another loss, another thing that's not me anymore."

"Being lesbian? You're not going to change that…"

"No, being in the closet. Yeah, you can't move much, it's hard to breathe, and you have to keep very quiet, but for all that the closet is a safe, comforting place. The sunlight is a lot more glaring, more revealing, than that single naked bulb. It's good to be out, but it's another trauma that I didn't need on top of the rape. I guess the best plus is that it's helping me find out who my friends are, like Alice. It's also given my enemies a double-barreled shotgun to point at me."

"Double-barreled?"

"Gay and raped. It must have been my fault. I don't need to hear them saying that, I'm having enough trouble hearing myself say it."

"Do you say it to your friends?"

"Yes."

"How do they respond?"

"The good ones let me say it, then help me know it's not true. The rest get demoted on my helper list. The ones who agree, the ones who are tired of hearing it, the ones who criticize me for even thinking it, the ones who plug their ears because somewhere inside they believe they could do something to get raped and don't want me to bring that to their consciousness."

"You seem very knowledgeable and perceptive."

"Alice has been a treasure. She not only went through it, she studied up on the recovery literature."

"It sounds like it, but in the end she'll probably reach a limit, too. Or you will. Has the counselor I work with been reaching out to you? You may not be ready for her now, but she'll keep in touch until you are."

"Yes. I keep thanking her for calling. I don't feel comfortable asking her to stop, or asking her why she keeps calling."

"For the same reason I keep calling. Because most survivors need to be offered help. They don't know where to look or even what they're looking for. They won't seek it out on their own, especially when they're in denial, and without help they may never get past denial."

"I think Alice said something like that. I have so much to learn about this recovery thing."

"And that's why the counselor and I will keep calling you. You don't have to learn how to do it. You just have to do it."

16 STRATEGY

Up on the tightrope
One side hate and one is hope

Dan hoped he was ready for this. He had the greeting sheet, and not much more, except for a knot in his stomach. "Let's start with introductions. Please share with us your name, one hope for today, one concern as we begin our process, and answer the question I posed on the greeting sheet: If you were a person, place, or thing in the Bible, what would it be? We don't need to go in order."

"I'll start. I'm Pastor Allen. My first thought is that this meeting is a logical inconsistency. I'm having a cognitive dissonance over it, and the reason for that is my main concern. As we go about this process we have to be totally transparent. Yet here we are having a secret meeting about how to do that. So my hope is that we can find a way to engage the whole church with the love of Christ and Christian caring for one another foremost in our hearts. My concern is that it is already too late, the lines have been drawn and we'll have a battle on our hands.

"Oh, and I would be Noah's ark, before the flood. With my doors open hoping everyone will come inside, but worried about the people and creatures who will be left out when the doors go shut."

"I'll go next. Hi, I'm Alice, and my hope for today is that we figure out how to start on the right foot. My concern is that the Annual Conference will find out what we're doing and send someone down to sit on us. And I would be Rachel: 'Wither thou goest I will go, and thy people will be my people.' That's a metaphor for what I had to say to Trevor when he stopped being Tina."

"Hi, I'm Dottie. My hope is that I'll be able to connect with all of you today. And as you probably can guess, that's not a given, especially for the men in the room. I'll try, but my concern is that something we talk about today will snap me right back to the … to a place I don't want to go. And I'd be one of the Sabine women – that is in the Bible, isn't it?"

"No, it isn't, but we'll give you a pass."

"Thanks, Pastor."

"Who wants to go next?"

"I'm Bill. My hopes and concerns I guess are pretty much the same as the others. The reason I'm here is that I think it's time for Third Methodist to address the gay issue, and I want to help this group get that started. And I wish we didn't have to go behind people's backs to figure out how to do that."

"And the question?"

"I forgot. Let's see… I think I would be water. Water parting to make way for something. I hope it's the water of the Jordan. If it's the water of the Red Sea, I hope we're Israel and not Pharaoh's chariots."

"Good afternoon, I'm Glenda. My hope for today is that we'll find enough love in this room that it will be an irresistible wave through the church. My concern is that the people we have here are all the support we're going to get. And I'd be Mary Magdalene."

"I guess I'm last. I'm Donna. I'd be Zacchaeus, the tax collector hiding in the tree, hoping for redemption but not feeling worthy. My hope is that I can find my divine spark that I've kept hidden for so long. And my concern is that if Mandy finds out I'm here she'll just pull in her head like a turtle and bring half the church with her."

"Thank you all. I'm Dan, and I'll be your facilitator today. It's my job to remain absolutely neutral as to the outcome of this meeting, but to be a real tyrant when it comes to the process we use and how we treat one another during the process. Which creates quite a conflict for me, too, Pastor Allen, because I care with equal passion about the process we use today and the process this church will use for this big decision, and how church members treat one another during that process, and those are the two things we're here to decide today. That means my process values lapse over into content values for today, and I'm not supposed to do that. So my hope is that I'll be able to help you all find a good process without unduly influencing exactly what that process is. My concern is that I'll fall off that tightrope and crash and burn. And my hope is that if I do, I do it spectacularly with a fire to light the January sky! My Bible character is the camel, trying desperately to make it through the eye of the needle."

"I have another concern I want to add."

"Go ahead, Dottie."

"I'm concerned that what we're up against is not bigotry but matters of faith, and that no matter how much love and understanding we show to others, they won't see any wiggle room in their reading of Scripture. Glenda talked about this the first time we talked to Alice, and I've been thinking about it."

"I'll add that to the list."

"Yes, Dottie, I remember saying that. Pastor Allen, what do you think?"

Time to start earning my keep, Dan thought. "Process check here. Is this how we want to proceed? Is everyone okay with talking about this one concern out of our whole list? I'm not against it, I just want to make sure it's a conscious choice that the group agrees with, not just a haphazard discussion."

"I think Dottie and Glenda hit the nail on the head. In spite of Pastor Allen's Christmas Eve discourse on Acts, Mandy is still hung up on Leviticus. Why is that?"

"I think I can speak to that, Donna."

"Is it okay with everyone else if Pastor Allen leads off on this topic?" Wait for it… "Silence is assent. Go ahead."

"Each of us has certain things we have to believe. We each take those have-to-believes and build a framework. Then everything else we come across either gets woven into that framework or, if it can't fit, it gets discarded. Only when you find something new, something that you have to believe and that doesn't fit, do you challenge the framework. If we're going to get Mandy and her crowd on board, we have to find something she *has* to believe in that will cause her to drop Leviticus out of the have-to-believe category and build a new framework. And I don't think Acts 8 is going to do it."

"I heard an interview with Utah State Senator Stuart Adams last summer. He's a Mormon who had a lot to do with Utah's Gay Rights laws. He talked about finally realizing his belief in loving everyone that God made trumped his religious beliefs about certain things being a sin. For some reason that interview came to mind during your Christmas Eve sermon. That's why I'm here. You and Senator Adams make a strong tag team."

"Thank you, Donna, I wondered what brought you here. I also wondered how you found out about this meeting, and no one else did."

"Well, Pastor, I started asking around. First I just asked 'what did you think of…?' questions, you know, just to gauge the reaction of people. I'm afraid that when I got negative responses, I didn't push back. I'm not very good at confrontation, I just made noncommittal monosyllabic noises and went on. I did have a couple of conversations with people who were on the fence, and since I was still pretty unsure myself we just did some exploration and some soul searching. Finally, when God thought I was ready, when I'd talked to enough 'maybe' people that I was starting to feel stronger about opening our doors to everyone, to living up to the 'Open hearts. Open minds. Open doors.' tag line, God sent me to Dan. He told me about this meeting and thought my viewpoint could be useful. So here I am."

"Well, thank you again for being here."

"Thank you for letting me in, Pastor."

"Okay, another process check. We've talked about belief structures, and I sense from the body language of those that haven't spoken that many think that our task is to create a process that recognizes the need for others to change their belief structures before they can change their minds. Is that a fair assessment? Are we close to consensus on that…? Thoughts…? Anyone?"

Honor the silence, Dan. Remember how long it can take people to decide to say something, to think through the ramifications and the inputs and the considerations. Honor the silence…

"I think the real issue is how do we get a process going to make Third Methodist a reconciling congregation."

"Thank you, Alice. What do others think? Glenda?"

"I think Alice is presuming an answer. "

"Let's keep this impersonal. Comment on the comment, not the speaker."

"I think that question presumes an answer. I think our goal is a process whereby Third Methodist can discern whether or not we will become a reconciling congregation, and our challenge is to find a way to do that that gives each member a chance to discern in their own heart how they feel about it."

"Dottie?"

"I think Glenda has a point. We have many good models here, people with ideas that can help. There's Pastor's divine spark. There's Senator Adams' coming to find that love trumps dogma. Especially helpful is Donna's example of engaging in open dialogue until she came to a solid understanding within herself – I think that has to be a key part of our strategy. But above all, I've been thinking about Dan's belief that the discernment process is more important than what's decided. We have to go into this trusting the process, and let the outcome be what it is."

"But doesn't that put us at an automatic disadvantage? The other side already knows what the answer is. They're not going to engage in discernment."

"I'm going to take off my facilitator hat and put on my participant hat. Alice, I hear what you're saying. A discernment process doesn't come easy to a lot of people. I remember the very first exercise I did as a facilitator trainee. It was a workshop at Coast Guard Headquarters. We started as we started today – with hopes and concerns. The very first person to speak was a crusty old Coast Guard chief petty officer, and he said, 'I hope we get done with this touchy-feely shit soon.' But we still have to trust the process, and trust that the Spirit will be moving in the process, in the same way that the eleven Apostles trusted the Spirit to guide them when they selected, who was it?, to replace Judas and round out the twelve."

"Matthias. Acts 1:26. 'And they gave forth their lots, and the lot fell upon Matthias.' But we've skipped verse 24: 'And they prayed and said, "Thou, Lord, which knowest all hearts, show us what You have chosen."' I think we all need to say a silent prayer, and each in our own heart ask for the guidance of our own God in words that make sense to us. Let's have a minute of silent prayer."

"Amen."

"Donna, then Alice."

"No, Alice, you go first."

"I'm a little disappointed, and a little chastened. I came here expecting this was the first step in getting Trevor and myself full acceptance into the church family. Now I'm hearing that that's not a foregone conclusion. And yet Glenda, and Dottie, and Pastor, and most of all Dan are right. If that's the conclusion going in, then we're not doing discernment, and it's never going to work. Thank you. I'm done with that."

"Donna?"

"I'd like to suggest something, and I can't believe I'm saying this. I must have prayed too hard. I think we should plan a congregational meeting to talk about a discernment process. I think the announcement of the meeting should say all the things that Glenda and Dottie just said about finding the answer, not moving toward a given answer.

"But Pastor was also right about being transparent. If we announce a congregational meeting in a vacuum, the other side is going to know this strategy meeting happened, so…whew…here goes nothing…I volunteer to go to Mandy and tell her we met *before* we go to church council and ask for a congregational meeting. If she feels blindsided it's just going to make it that much harder to win her over."

"Thank you, Donna." *Man, after she said that, she just kind of deflated, and put her hands in her lap. She looks like she's trying to keep from shaking.*

I love Mandy, Donna thought. *Mandy was like a big sister to me when I came to this church, fresh out of my first marriage to that son of a…to that abusive man. She introduced me to people, well, to all the 'right' people, but still she was concerned for me, in her own way, and made me feel welcome. I love Mandy. I hope I love her enough to pull this off. I'll find out tomorrow.*

17 DONNA AND MANDY

Like a bridge over troubled waters I will lay me down

"Donna, hello, come in, I didn't expect to see you this morning. What are you up to?"

"Mandy, there's something I wanted to talk to you about, and I didn't want to do it on the phone."

"This sounds serious. Come on in. Is everything okay? Is it Peter or one of the girls?"

"Thank you. No, everyone's okay. This is church business."

"Sit down. Can I get you something? Coffee, water, sweet tea? Oh, I forget I'm in New England and no one up here drinks sweet tea in January."

I'd better not start something I may not get a chance to finish. "Let's wait awhile. This might be a short conversation. If you don't throw me out, I might take something later."

"Now you really have me worried." *Church business. It's got to be this whole issue about the queers. I wonder if she's heard something? Something new? How could she hear something I haven't heard?* "What's this about?"

"Mandy, a lot of people at Third Methodist think it's time to have a discussion about whether or not we are being called to become a reconciling congregation..."

I knew it. "No Way I'm going to let a bunch of those people…"

"Now hold on. We already have a bunch of 'those people' in our church. And I didn't say 'Let them in.' We want to discuss whether or not we are being called…"

"You're one of them? Do you want to go against the *Book of Discipline* and say that twisted lifestyle is okay?"

"No, I want – we want – the church to have an open discussion, and I wanted you to hear it from me first. We want to bring the issue out in the open and give the Spirit a chance to speak through each of us, for everyone to hear from both sides…"

"I don't need two sides. I don't need the Spirit. I've got the Bible and the *Book of Discipline* and that settles it."

"But what about open hearts open minds open doors? The United Church of Christ says, 'God is still speaking…'"

"Those damned Yankee Congregationalists. What would they know? Did you know that sometimes they even leave out verses when they're singing hymns?"

"So do we sometimes."

"And Pastor Allen hears from me every time we do, you can count on that!"

I'm sure I can. How did I not notice this side of Mandy before? But I still love her…I think. "Can we get back to the issue at hand?" *It's a good thing I didn't ask for coffee. Her old percolator would be jumping off the stove by now. I was hoping we would have a rational discussion. I don't see it going that way.* "Let me start over. A group of church members met with Pastor to talk about this issue. I convinced them…"

"You were there? As a spy for them or a double agent for us?"

"I'm hoping there's not going to be an 'us' and 'them.' I convinced them to ask the Church Council for an open, transparent process of discernment with no foregone conclusion. The world is changing and we, as a church, need to be ready with a response, whatever that is going to be.

And we want you to have a voice in that process."

"You want to co-opt me, you mean. Nothing doing. They may have gotten to you, but they're not going to get to me. I know my Bible. I'm not one of those cafeteria Christians. I don't pick and choose what commandments I want to follow."

"And that's why we need you. A lot of people feel the way you do, but yours is the most powerful voice of that viewpoint. We don't want this to be a steamroller or a rubber stamp. We want room for every voice, every consideration and concern. We want to start the process with everyone operating out of Christian love for everyone else." *Let's see her wriggle out of that one. I bet she'll try. Oh, Donna, trapping Mandy with the 'Christian love' gambit isn't Christian love.* "So can we plan on you for the first meeting?"

"Damn right I'll be there! I'll be there to shut the whole thing down. I've got the Bible and I've got the *Book of Discipline.*"

"Do what you have to do. I don't think you'll be able to stop the process, and I'm hoping you'll be able to open your heart to at least hear everyone. You used to care a lot about Alice. She used to be one of us. She's still the same person."

"One of us? After going to the enemy's meeting and bringing their message to me, to throw in my face, do you think *you* are still 'one of us'?"

"I guess I'd better be going. I'll take a rain check on that coffee."

"And it will be a cold day in Hell when you get it!" *The nerve of her! Coming in here to ask me to vote for letting faggots and dykes have the run of the church! I showed her! Time to get on the phone again.* She wondered, though…who could she still trust?

18 GEORGE

I'm a runnin' down the road tryin' to loosen my load
Got a world of trouble on my mind

George stood by the statue in Winslow. He had had to get out of Dodge – or whatever Berkshire town was a stand in for Dodge. It got too hot for him. Who ever said that most rape victims never report it? None of the girls he got drunk at Junior College had ever spilled, but that lesbo dyke bitch slut had what he and the boys did all over the newspapers in half of three states, and some big-market local TV stations besides. It never occurred to him that leaving her with no means of survival except to call 911 kind of reduced her opportunity to not call the police.

When he had found out about the roofie dealer, he knew just what he wanted to do. He scored the pills, only two, that's all that The Pharmacist would sell him, before he started planning his play. Then he recruited some friends. If he was going to pull this off, he'd need someone to drop the pill while he distracted the mark, and to help her out to the four-by when she was drifting off, and to get her out of it when she was gonzo. Plus, he had to have more than just him to assault her to confuse the DNA trail. So he befriended those Berkshire Mountain Men.

107

What a laugh. Go to work in jackets and ties, then change into jeans and flannel to do their drinking like they were from the real Appalachia. Got 'em talking about what if and wouldn't you like to know what happened when and boy what I wouldn't give to be able to, and he had them.

Now to nail down the subject.

He'd had his suspicions about those two women roommates, the ones who shared the house that was on his usual route. He started hanging around. He didn't want to know their names. He just called them "Slim" and "Big Butt." Eastwick was on the mailbox, but he didn't know whether that was the family name of Big Butt or Slim, and he didn't want to know.

Slim and Big Butt were real careful in public, but in their yard they got real lovey-dovey. He'd even played peeping Tom a few times and caught them kissing and grabbing ass while they cooked. They were both a little long in the tooth. Big butt, the one from the museum, was a little, ah, Rubenesque to say the least. Slim was lean and mean. He'd go for Slim in a heartbeat, but Big Butt would feel good, too, and might be more grateful for the favor they were going to do her.

He started watching their movements. Start of November, Slim's schedule changed. Must have to do with the size of the crowds at the bed and breakfast, now that the colors were gone. Big Butt would come in to Lenox for a coffee at *Get Lit* and wait for Slim to get off work. So he and the boys started hanging around. They started paying attention to all the women in the place. They boys didn't know it was Big Butt that he had his eye on.

Then, on Thanksgiving, he had noticed that most of the Eastwick house was dark but there was a glow in the backyard. He snuck around back. Bingo! Naked as the day they were born, snuggling before the fire, watching a movie with that limey fagot Hugh Grant. Naked! Displaying it all, just for him!

He decided that he wouldn't let another month go by.

The roofies were burning a hole in his pocket. He made a date with the boys for December 1. Snow was predicted; that would help cover their tracks. He headed for Lenox and *Get Lit*, but Big Butt wasn't there! He asked around – discretely. Someone said she hadn't been in for a couple of days. Didn't like how rowdy the place had gotten. They cruised the sidewalks a bit. There, in the café right around the corner! The boys seemed a little surprised and disappointed with Big Butt and her middle-aged wrinkles and her middle-aged waistline, but he bluffed his way through. He pointed out her big boobs, and the big ass that he knew would appeal to at least one of them. People were so easy to manipulate.

Like that waiter and all the people drinking their coffee. He managed to convince them that Big Butt was his friend. They believed because they wanted to believe. It was the story that was to their advantage. They believed him because it was easier than believing that something was going on that they should get involved in. They wanted George to make whatever was going on come out all right. A couple 'a bitches looked a little uncertain, but George knew just when to turn on the charm and just when to give the 'I-dare-you-to-say-anything' glare.

Everything had gone according to plan. She hadn't been awake for any of it. They didn't do anything beyond what could be construed as rough sex. No restraints, no marks, didn't even steal anything except her panties, and how many women had their panties torn in the throes and then ditched them before going home to hubby, or Mom? A lot, judging by the number of pairs he found when he was jogging around the back roads.

But then she showed up in the papers. Had to be her, even without a name or a picture. The description of the crime was too perfect. They might as well just have called the victim Big Butt. He knew they were talking about her, about the boys, about him.

And to top it all off, one of them – he called himself

'Dick' – had confessed! Now the heat was going to be ten times hotter. Ten times hotter, what did that even mean? Why had he thought of that old Bible passage and the fight with his mother? Was it Daniel that the king heated the oven ten times hotter for? No, Daniel went to the lions. It was those other three, Sad Sack, Midrash, and To Bed We Go, or something like that. When he first heard the story, he tried to figure it out. Let's see, he said to his mom, how hot is your oven? Figure 350. Ten times as hot would be 3500. Not bloody likely, just another one of those Bible stories that couldn't be true. His mother had insisted that God could make it that hot, but it wasn't God who made it that hot, it was the King's men. Mom still washed his mouth out with soap for his blasphemy. Silly bitch. He'd gotten away from her as quick as he could.

He ditched the second roofie somewhere in the panhandle. Waited for the blonde at the end of the lunch counter to head for the ladies room. He threw a ten on the table for his tab and dropped the pill in the bitch's coffee as he left. Maybe it took effect before she got in her car to drive. He hadn't heard about any fiery crash on the Amarillo eleven o'clock news that night. Boy, would she have some 'splainin' to do when she woke up, and absolutely no memory of anything to go on. Her husband, or boyfriend, or girlfriend, probably wasn't buying any of it. Bitch deserved it, the haughty way she flounced her hair and turned away when all he had done was give her his best smile.

Boy, I wish I knew The Pharmacist's real name. *The Eagle* said that Dick's confession had reinforced the view held by the police that 'the rash of rohypnol-related assaults' were all attributable to one dealer. The press called him 'The Pharmacist.' Half the state of Massachusetts was looking for him. If the fuzz ever catch me, I'd sure like to be able to give him up to get some leverage. That ought to buy me something for my own case, as bad as they want him. I never forget a face, though. If they have him in their mug shot books, I'll nail him.

Damn, I've got to change some things. Dick didn't give them a thing on me, but Big Butt remembers a cowboy hat, fancy boots, and a big belt buckle. She can't remember enough to describe any of them, but by now one of those meddling bitches from the café has probably come forward, and without the roofie she probably gave a decent account, but if I ditch the hat, boots, and buckle out here, people will start to figure I'm not from around here and that would be even more suspicious. Maybe just change the hat. People around here would recognize the description of the hat. Belt buckle can go in my luggage. It's too hard to break in a new pair of boots. Damn, it was a brand new Stetson, too. 30X. Set me back more than the roofies. Will people notice if I get a new one? Will that call even more attention to it? I'm overthinking this, second guessing myself. I'm still on the move. I'll just go to Tractor Supply, get me a cheap straw work hat. Then once I'm back on the road, I'll put on the straw hat and put the Stetson in the trunk. Gotta settle in the next town and find some work. At least I can use my real name and social. The Berkshire cops don't have that – yet.

19 THERE OUGHTA BE A WORD

It's sad, so sad, why can't we talk it over
Always seems to me sorry seems to be the hardest word

Dottie was having another down day. At least she was starting to put her finger on what was missing. She wasn't confronting her emotions. She kept telling the story of *what* happened. As hard as it was to relive the night, that was really the easy part. She knew *what* happened to her, she could repeat the story, but her feelings, her emotions, her reactions, those were harder. She couldn't share with others what she couldn't sort out for herself. Being dragged back to the events was hard enough. Being forced to confront what was still inside her as a result of what happened scared the hell out of her. She *really* didn't want to go there. She felt conflicted, pulled apart between her modern-woman beliefs and the old stigma. In her mind she was an innocent victim and a guilty collaborator at the same time. *I can't sort them out. I don't want to go there.* When she told Alice what she was afraid of, she left out the part about the inner war. She was too afraid of that, of going there, to even name it. She was afraid that if she tried to talk this out with Alice, or Mary, or Glenda, it would be too scary for them, too, and she'd drive them away. *So I'm pulling away instead. At least they're not being pushy. They're giving me space. And time.*

Alice felt it too. *Dottie has something she needs to talk about, I can tell, but she won't bring it up with me.* She didn't know if it was too scary for Dottie or if Dottie thought it would be too scary for Alice. *She has to know that all of us in her support group are ready to hear whatever has to come out. I hope she's not interpreting space as inability to deal.* Alice was starting to think that it fell to her to make the first move. She had never been exactly where Dottie was, but she'd been through the neighborhood, and that's closer than Glenda or Mary, and Dottie had never before been where she was now, either; the first time is the hardest. *I don't know where I'd be today if Joan hadn't gotten me to open up about my rape – and Kris before her getting me to talk about Trevor. I'm going over.*

"Dottie, can I come in?"

"Alice, of course, always. How are you? What brings you down this way?"

"I want to talk to you. No, I want you to talk to me. If you want to talk I am willing and available to listen. To anything. I assume, even two months after, that you still have some, many, unresolved feelings. I've been feeling really helpless. I can see you're in pain and struggling with your feelings, and I don't know how to respond. I'm afraid of pushing you too far. I don't know exactly where you are, how tough or vulnerable you are at this point, how ready or scared or neither or both you are to bring it out. I won't push now, either, but I had to let you know I'm here, I'm listening, and I need you to trust me to let you know when I've had too much and need a time out. I won't break. I'll take care of myself, but I want you to take care of you, and I want you to know I'm here to listen if it will help. We can keep dancing around each other, or we can talk. I'm still here. I'm still listening."

She's right, of course. We're in stalemate, and I'm in horrible conflict and don't know what to do about it. So I think I'll open a bottle of wine. My dad always bought time when he needed to think by filling, tamping, and lighting his pipe. Wine is my preferred gambit.

"Shall we drink it here in the kitchen or take it in the family room? Or in the living room? We hardly ever use the living room."

"Wherever you're comfortable." *We're going to talk about some uncomfortable things, I hope. She has to be comfortable to do that, but comfortable as in 'half reclining on an overstuffed sofa clutching a throw pillow' or comfortable as in 'sitting in a warm, friendly, familiar kitchen on a good, supportive chair at a communal table'? Her call.*

Dottie thought about it. *The living room has never felt like mine. The kitchen is for talking over coffee.* "Let's take it into the family room." *That may not be the best place either; that's Glenda's and my place because of how our relationship formed, was lived out, and has changed there, but hey.* "Will you grab the bottle?"

That's a good sign. She thinks this is going to be more than a one-glass conversation, and by asking me to pick up the bottle, she's giving me a chance to vote in the affirmative. "Got it. Lead the way."

Dottie played a few opening gambits in her head. *How do I start? Where do I begin? Well, when it's hard to start, that's a good place to start – with why it's hard.* "I really don't know where to begin. I'm really struggling with a lot of competing emotions. This is the 21st century, I'm a liberated woman. I've read Betty Friedan and Gloria Steinem and Erica Jong. I know this was not my fault, I know it was equal parts those men and the patriarchal, male-dominated, fucked-up society we live in. I know I should cry 'RAPE!' at the top of my lungs, but I keep hearing the voices of my youth, the ones that say it's the woman's fault, it's the fault of all women, it's my fault. That we ask for it, that we make ourselves vulnerable, that we send mixed signals. How can all that crap still be in my head in this day and age? I'm so ashamed of it being in there, but I can't get it out. If I could just believe it, I'd accept the blame and move on, but I can't accept it and I can't shake it."

"Stupid, silly, bigoted ideas like that are gifts we're given as children, and we spend the rest of our lives unlearning them. I'm still listening."

"I can't sleep. I always slept on my back, but when I lie on my back, I remember waking up on my back and realizing where I was and what had happened. I can't sleep on my side or on my stomach either – that's not how I sleep. And when I *do* fall asleep and wake up on my back, it's even worse. It's not just remembering, I'm there again. I'm surprised when I finally realize I'm under the covers, I'm not exposed, I'm not alone, and it's not snowing, but the panic is still there, the heart is still running a sprint, and I'm wide awake. It's more real than it was that night, because then I was still drowsy and drugged and foggy and forgetting. Now it's all right there, in sharp focus, getting sharper with every repeat.

"The nightmares are still there, when I do sleep. Even though I heard Dick's confession, even though the uncertainty is over, the nightmares keep morphing and multiplying. The things they could have done to me. The ways they could have hurt me. All the reasons they might have had to kill me. All the stories of what has happened to other women are just the start. I take all of them and combine them, embellish them, make them more extreme. The Woman who Lost her Village…"

"From *The Vagina Monologues?*"

"That's the one. I don't know how she survived, kept any sanity, and yet some of my dreams are even more extreme. It's only because they gradually fade as the light of day reminds me what is real, and because Glenda holds me, that I can maintain any grip on reality. Then I remember the reality, and that reality is bad enough for anyone.

"Which leaves me caught in another mental conflict. I know other women have had it worse, other women have been killed, other women have killed themselves in shame, or been mutilated or killed by the men in their family for bringing dishonor. I feel guilty to be alive, to be making such a big deal over one evening, but if I don't acknowledge that something terrible happened to me, it's like excusing them, like I'm giving them a bye. I have a right to be angry, and scared, and in pain over what they took from me. On top of it all, I don't even know what to call what they took from me."

"That's the kicker, isn't it? It's been almost four years since my rape, and whatever it is that my rapist took, I still haven't gotten it back. A lot of people, people who have never had it taken from them, especially men, think that rape is less serious than the theft of something tangible, than losing your stuff. It's not. It's much bigger. It's only the tiniest little bit less than murder. We *don't* have a word for what is taken from us in rape, but the only thing more intimate, more personal, more important, more irreplaceable is a life. We need a name for this thing, so we can talk about it, understand it, learn about the pain that comes when it is lost."

"Sometimes I feel like I did lose my life, and my soul. Maybe that's what they took. Or maybe it's my freedom."

"It's big parts of all of those things, and a lot of other things like sense of safety and peace and joy. It's our power and our control and our self worth, our self identity. We can wrap a whole bunch of things in the word 'life' and know that that is what is taken from us in death. We need a word that wraps up everything that is taken from us by rape. What is that thing? What word covers it all?"

"I don't know, but I think one of my rapists, Dick, the one who confessed, almost gets it. I think the reason he turned himself in is because George took a small part of that thing away from him, and that made Dick somewhat aware of what he took from me, and even though he could never give back what he took or get back what George took, he did the only thing he could do."

Dottie and Alice talked for a long time. They talked

through another whole bottle of wine. They drank slowly, so they could still make sense and be in touch with their emotions, and they drank steadily so that the inhibitions of the old taboos and learned behaviours didn't get in the way of their sharing.

They talked until they fell into each other's arms, crying – and laughing. They laughed because they were in that place where it feels so good to finally bring all the bad feelings to the surface where you can actually feel them, own them, cry over them, deal with them.

When Glenda came home, they talked some more. They drank some more. Dottie got some cheese and crackers and veggie sticks from the kitchen with the next bottle of wine, and they ate as they drank. They drank until all three of them agreed that Alice had best not drive home.

"The guest room is available again. Dottie has moved all her stuff back into our room. Why don't you stay over? Trevor is back at school, isn't he? You can just call your husband and tell him you're fine and you'll be home in the morning."

"Huh. That would be quite a trick, calling my husband."

"What's his name? Joe? I think that's what I saw come up on caller ID: 'Douglas, Joseph'."

"Well, the phone's still in his name. He and his new girlfriend don't have a land line, so he left mine in his name. He still pays the bill – that was part of the settlement – but we haven't been together for, let's see, almost three years now."

"Oh, Alice, we didn't know. What happened?"

"I got raped. It made him feel like less of a man. First his beautiful little girl wanted to be a boy, then he couldn't keep his wife safe. Then he told the old joke about when rape is inevitable lie back and enjoy it, and I shut down. I couldn't trust him. I couldn't talk to him. I know now that he didn't mean it, that it came from a dark place where his feelings of inadequacy took him, and the only light he could see was the old stereotype. The rape affected him, too, and he was struggling, but we just couldn't struggle together, and struggling with each other on top of all the other stresses was just more than either one of us could do. So we split. You two are so lucky that you found your way back to each other."

"Alice, we just didn't know. You've been so supportive of me, such a friend to Glenda, and we never even asked about your life, your rape, your struggles. How could we have been so insensitive?"

"Don't give it another thought. You didn't know because I didn't tell you. I told you about the rape up front because it helped you accept me as someone who has been there. I told you about Trevor up front because it helped you accept me as not totally in Mandy's camp. If you two had started having problems, I would have told you about Joe and me to get conversation started to help you there, too. Except, of course, Joe and I would have been the counterexample."

"Bullshit. You're not just an example, you're a human being. You have your right to your own struggles, and we weren't tuned in. We were no help. We just let you listen while Dottie and I ran on and on."

"Dottie, do you remember when I told you that you needed friends who would love you more than themselves? I tried to be that friend. Of course you were both a big help to me. Glenda, you saw what Dottie and I were doing when you came in. Dottie and I had been talking about feelings we both have had, both of us were letting out things that had been bottled up. Then when you joined, we talked some more and broke bread together and moved from support system to friends. And now, as friends, you're letting me talk about the other things that are in my life, and not in my life anymore. And now I think that I will stop drinking – before I make an utter fool of myself – and start thinking about sleeping in a bed before I pass out right here."

"The bed's made. There's toothpaste and a new tooth-brush in the medicine chest and clean towels on the towel bar. Dottie and I each put some of our old pajamas in the top dresser drawer."

"I think Glenda's will probably fit you better than mine. What do you like for breakfast? What time do you need to get out of here in the morning?"

"Juice, decaf, a little toast. And I'm not on a schedule. What time to do you need to get rid of me?"

"Nothing pressing, and if you think you're going to get out of the house of a bed and breakfast owner with just a little toast, you're seriously mistaken. Besides, we may want to talk some more. So breakfast will be at 7:30."

Group hug.

Fade to black.

20 INTEGRATION

Do you think I'd crumble
Did you think I'd lay down and die?
Oh no, not I, I will survive
Oh, as long as I know how to love, I know I'll stay alive

"I probably should have come to see you long before this."

"There is no 'should'. Take that word out of your vocabulary, along with 'must', 'need to', and 'have to'. You choose what's right for you. You balance the benefits, risks, and consequences and you make your choice. That's important to understand in daily living. It's essential in healing."

"You mean I must take 'must' out of my vocabulary?"

"Touché. It is very helpful in life and healing. Because everyone heals at their own pace, in their own order. If you start thinking you should have done something long ago just to keep up with some imagined timetable or someone else's schedule, you just add more stress. You might beat yourself up over it. You might even set yourself back. Not that it's bad to go back and redo if something feels incomplete, but if your goal is to move forward, to get past, then it might be good to avoid words, thoughts, and people that make that difficult, that set you back more than you would be without them. I'm not saying this very well."

"No, that makes sense, in a scary kind of way."

"Why scary?"

"Because Professor Irwin Corey used to make sense to me. It's freaky when you can understand what is supposed to sound like gibberish. Oops, is 'supposed to' a banned word?"

"I don't know if I've just been complimented or insult-ed."

"Sorry, neither one, I'm just babbling. You must get that a lot in first sessions."

"At any rate this isn't about me, it's about you. I should... it would be good if I let you talk and keep my own stuff for me."

"No, I wouldn't trust you if I didn't feel you were being authentic with me. I remember a workshop where we were talking about values. I said one of mine was authenticity. Everyone else in the room looked at me like I was crazy. To them it's all about keeping your agenda, your concerns, your Self hidden."

"Authenticity is important to you, then?"

"Yes, I have to be authentic. Sorry, I value being au-thentic. 'To thine own self be true' and all that. I guess that's why it was so hard not being out to so many peo-ple."

"Interesting. We may get back to that. So tell me, Dot-tie, after all the times I called you, why come to me now?"

"I thought I could do this myself. I thought I had a good support network and we would get through this."

"And it's not happening?"

"Well, here's how it went. I told my story a lot of times, to a lot of people. Some didn't want to hear it, or made jokes about it, or held me at arm's length. Some talked a good game up front, but turned out to be 'those people' who knew what's best for me and told me what the steps were and when I should be finished. Yeah, I guess you're right, 'should' is a dirty word. Some were great for a while, but grew tired or ran out of energy. The best ones are Alice and Glenda and Mary. They're still sticking with me but they realize – I realize – that they don't have the chops – I guess that's the word – to help me get all the way past. Especially Alice. She said she didn't want to be Obi Wan."

"Obi Wan? In what way?"

"You remember. In episode four, Obi Wan Kenobi admits that he thought he could train Anakin just because he'd been through the Jedi training himself, but his learning experience wasn't enough to make him an adequate teacher. Alice said she started out by thinking her experience with recovery would be all I needed, but she told me she was only deluding herself."

"Why did she say that?"

"Because I've stopped getting better. I can go to work, but I have to keep my shifts short or the anxiety starts to build into a panic. I have trouble with the Q&A portion of my gallery talks, especially when it's a guy asking the question. A lot of things still snap me back, and I still have the nightmares."

"That's a lot of issues all at once. Are they all stable?"

"What do you mean? What is stable about any of that? It all feels like I'm pretty unstable."

"I mean the symptoms themselves. Do you always start to panic after exactly the same number of hours at the museum? Is it always the fourth question that makes you panic? Do you always have two nightmares a night and three snap-backs a week?"

"No,... but,...I don't know, I haven't counted or anything, but they're always there."

"Do you have good days and bad days? Bad days and worse days?"

"Yes, of course, but…"

"But what?"

"But it doesn't seem to be getting any better."

"Did you ever watch waves at the seashore? Some

waves come in further than others. You have to watch dozens or even hundreds of waves before you can see if the tide is coming in or going out. Now look back over the last week, the last month. Is the tide coming in or going out?"

"Which is good and which is bad?"

"You tell me."

"It's coming in. Slowly, but it's flowing in. And I'm stuck on the beach. I'm paralyzed like when they drugged me, but still conscious this time, and I feel like I'm going to drown because the water is rising and I can't move. That's why I came to you now. I survived the rape. I survived the hospital. My relationship with Glenda survived – did I tell you we're getting married? I even survived coming out at church. I survived the phase of moping around the house in pajamas. I survived, but I'm not healing. The wound is still draining and won't form a scar. I don't think I could have sought help until I was sure I would survive, but now that I know, I need help to live."

"Without passing judgement, that sounds like a pretty good place to be. Now, in what way do you think you need help?"

"Think! I *know* I need help!! Sorry, that was uncalled for. It happens a lot. I know it's important to figure out who I can count on and who will not be supportive, but I get hypercritical. I lash out at the slightest lapse, like when I tell Mary I don't want coffee but she brings it anyway. She thinks she's helping. I see it as taking away my freedom, of overriding my decision. I've lost so much, and so much of what I've lost is my freedom, my power, my sense of control. That's maybe where I need help. I still feel like my life is out of control, like it's not mine anymore. So much is missing."

"Bill Bridges has an interesting outlook on loss. He draws a distinction between grieving and mourning. Grieving is the intense emotion you feel when you lose something. Mourning is a process. It's building your life in a new way, a way that accounts for the missing things and finds things to replace them. I can be your guide through that process, but you have to do the rebuilding."

"It's like that old riddle, huh? 'How many therapists does it take to change a lightbulb? Can't be done, the lightbulb has to want to change itself.' So where do we begin?"

"I don't think we just jump in. *You* start off by being clear about what you've lost, what parts of your life you need to rebuild. Some of your losses may even need some more grieving. Then you have to be clear about the things that are now part of you that you never wanted. You've been raped. That experience is now a part of you. You have to make it a smaller and smaller part, but you also have to build defenses around it to protect yourself because it's never going to go away."

"That's an awful lot of 'need's and 'have to's."

"Let me reword it. You can choose to rebuild your life and get better, or you can choose to get worse. I can almost guarantee that the tide will either come in or go out. If you choose to get better, then there are actions that are essential to your process."

"Fair enough. So what's your role while I'm doing all this essential work?"

"I'm your focal point. I'm your schedule. I'm your sounding board. You can think about the things I mentioned over and over. You can make lists of answers and questions, you can write it all down in your journal along with thoughts and reactions and raw emotion. But many people – some would say most people – wont' have the focus to actually make progress that way. You'll spin your wheels thinking the same things over and over. You'll make a list of things lost and things added but won't address any of them. You'll avoid asking yourself the hard questions, being honest about the negative feelings, being impartial in evaluating your answers and your progress. It's a lot harder to lie to yourself when someone else is listening.

"And I'm talking too much. We've been at this for some time now and you haven't talked much. I'm going to ask those questions again. Then I'm just going to let you talk. Don't worry about being organized or remembering everything you say, I'll be taking notes and will use them to keep us on track. Ready? What have you lost?"

"Well, like I said, power, control, freedom. I've lost the freedom to walk the street without fear. I now know that rape *can* happen to me, and that really changes my feeling about being a woman. I don't feel predisastered. I know that my chances of being raped are the same as they were before I was raped, and now I know that those chances aren't as low as I thought. The statistics caught up with me, and they could again. I can no longer pretend I'm special, that some guardian angel is going to make me the exception. That's what I've lost, my guardian angel, and a little bit – maybe a big bit – of my faith went with her. I've lost my whole rosy world view. No amount of 'Life is Good' merchandise is going to make me believe it again. I thought I was in control of my own destiny. If I'm not in control of that, then I'm not in control of anything, and if I'm not in control, what am I doing?"

"Your whole life, your whole world, is tied up in being in control? Sounds like a real Type A, and I wouldn't have figured you for being that anal retentive."

"I wouldn't have either, but I have to believe that my choices make a difference. I only have two alternatives. Either my choices didn't matter, or my choices led to my rape and it's my fault. It's hard to live with either one of those ideas."

"Does it have to be either/or? Is there a third alternative? Can it be both/and? I'll let you think about that before our next session. In the meantime, consider that maybe none of us can control what happens outside of us, only what happens inside.

"I have a follow-up question. The freedom, the sense

of control, the guardian angel, the piece of your faith – where are you on grieving each of those losses?"

"What do you mean?"

"Losing anything is a little death. Losing big things like that are not-so-little little deaths, and little death goes through the same stages as Big Death, the ones Kübler-Ross outlined in *On Death and Dying*. For each thing you lose, you will go through denial, anger, bargaining, depression, and acceptance. Not necessarily linearly, but skip any of them and your psyche will take you back. I have a personal notion that maybe that's what a lot of rubber-banding – what you call 'snapping back' – is about. You can be pulled back to unwelcome feelings because you never really finished feeling them – not all the way. So where are you? Did you do denial?"

"There was a lot of denial. Maybe there still is. I tried to deny that being raped was going to change my life. Even when I was moping around the house in my pajamas, I was telling myself that tomorrow I would bounce back and be my old self again. Even when I couldn't share a room with Glenda, I kept promising myself that she and I would get back to the way we were.

"To believe I wasn't going to be affected by the rape, a part of me had to deny that it even happened. Before I knew what happened while I was knocked out, before Dick made his confession, even when I was making up horrible scenarios to fill in the gap, part of me was believing that all I did was take a nap. I kept thinking that pretty soon I'd wake up from one of my nightmares and find out the whole thing was dream, like Bobby Ewing getting shot."

"And just because you've done denial doesn't mean you won't ever have to do it again. What else?"

"Anger. Lots of anger. I've told my story to a lot of people. It's a good way to find out who is going to be useful. If they take the story onboard, take a part of the burden of my experience onto themselves, then they go on the 'ally' list, but others I often get angry with. Unreasonably so, when it wasn't them I was angry with."

"You were projecting. Who were you mad at?"

"Well, the guys, obviously. What names did Dick give for them? Tom, Dick, Harry, and George? Real original."

"Who else?"

"What do you mean?"

"Who else are you angry with? What else pisses you off and who do you blame for it?"

"The people in the café. Dick came right out and said that they let George intimidate them into doing nothing. The church ladies who blame me for being raped and for being a lesbian. Oh, yeah, that's something else I lost – the protection of my closet. The privacy. The right to choose who I tell and what I tell about me."

"And who are you angry at about that?"

"Myself, I guess. Sheri for calling Mandy – Sheri was my rape counselor at the hospital who called the church and Mandy is the woman who came to the hospital and badgered me till I blurted out the wrong thing."

"Are you still angry?"

"I'll always be angry at the four men, and at the culture that raised them, the culture that doesn't protect women."

"Can you do anything positive with that energy?"

"Like what?"

"Become an activist. Become an advocate. Write a book. Push for legislation. Push for education. Tell your story. You tell me."

"Be an example. Of what can happen, of what it means, of someone who is a person, not an object, not a victim, not a statistic. Not just a pawn in the war of the sexes."

"Sounds like a good start."

"I'm also pissed as hell at my guardian angel. Where was she when I needed her? Why did she fly away and let me lose my faith, along with everything else?"

"Talk more about your faith."

"I used to think I was special. That God was always looking out for me. Other kids lost their parents. I still had four grandparents and three greats. Other families had accidents and sickness. Ours never did. We were marked for good luck. Almost like I had been bred for good luck."

"I read a novel with a character like that."

"*Ringworld*? Great book. Larry Niven is the best. But I thought that about myself long before I read it. I 'knew' nothing bad would ever happen to me. Everyone I loved would die peacefully at a ripe old age, everything would work out fine."

"Did it?"

"Up to a point. My grandparents died of natural causes at fairly ripe old ages. My favorite aunt died much too young, but she lived far away, so I was always missing her, and that didn't change much when she died. Tragedies came, but each in a form I could handle, so they didn't really shake my optimism. In fact they made my faith stronger. I truly believed that old tripe that God never gives you more than you can handle. In the tough times, like when snow collapsed our garage roof and we were wading around in icy water up to our knees trying to save things, God felt closer than ever.

"But God wasn't with me when I woke up on October Mountain. God wasn't with me at that café in Lenox. God didn't prevent George from buying those roofies, or Tom Dick and Harry from raping me. So where was He?"

"Maybe She felt just as hurt, and angry, and sad, and violated as you."

"Bullsh…wait, what do you mean?"

"What do you think I mean?"

"I don't know. That God's not a man, that God doesn't,…that God wouldn't,…that…I don't know."

"Think about it. I feel like you've gotten in touch with a lot for today and this is a good place to pause. Like that god that you don't believe in anymore, I try to never give you more than you can handle – until it's time to overload you to break down a belief that isn't serving you well anymore, so you can find a different way to handle it. So I'll see you next Thursday. Meanwhile keep thinking about what you are grieving and what stages you've at least made a start on. Now give me a hug. You're strong, and you make me proud to be a woman."

21 THE COURTROOM

I fought the law and the law won

Susan took what she had to the Chief. "I think we have a line on George. A woman in Amarillo passed out at a bar. She was suspicious, and so were the authorities, so she got a blood test. Rohypnol."

"So? Aren't there like a thousand cases a year?"

"Not as many as you might think, and in this case their lab turned up a curious impurity, the stuff was probably homemade, and none of the other cases in the Southwest had that impurity, so they started looking wider. Heard about the rash of drug-involved sexual assaults in our area and contacted us. We looked at the samples from Dottie's case and the same impurity was there, at the same level. As good as a fingerprint."

"Okay, it's from the same source as our pharmacist uses. How does it tie in to George?"

"The lady remembers a cowboy at the other end of the bar making eyes at her. Thought he was God's gift to women. She didn't give him the time of day. Went to powder her nose and when she got back he was gone. Bartender says he noticed him, too, and that he seemed to pause by her stool on the way out."

"Still, cowboys must be a dime a dozen out there. Why do you think it's our cowboy?

"Both the lady and barkeep said he didn't fit. The clothes weren't right. And he took his hat off in the bar. Real Texas cowboys don't do that. And it was the wrong hat. He was wearing work clothes that didn't look worked in. He didn't look worked in. And the hat was a 30X Stetson. Should have been worn with a suit. A banker's hat. She picked it out of Cavender's catalogue. El Patron Silver Belly Felt. So now we have a description of the hat."

"Good. Get a picture of it, and some other hats. Do a photo lineup for the vic. See if it rings any bells. See if she can pick it out. What else?"

"Remember Dottie talked about a big belt buckle and fancy boots? The bartender got a good look at the buckle – silver and gold, just like Dottie said. Bartender had seen it before, on line, also at Cavender's. Silver and Gold Bull Rider Antique Buckle. $48.00. Silver and gold antique my ass. Sorry, Chief."

"Okay, get on that, too. Same drill as the hat. And now we know where he shops. Any description?"

"Five foot eight, medium build, middle aged, Caucasian, pale, like he spent some cold months up north. Could be anyone, but now that we have a tie in, maybe we could get the Amarillo police to ask the witnesses to spend some time with a forensic artist."

"I'll handle that directly. Chief to chief. Get me the results of the hat and buckle lineup ASAP, so I have a little more ammunition. Good work, Susan. One thing bothers me, though. Didn't Dick say George only had one pill?"

"One pill that he knew about. Here's the way I see it. George was holding out on them. Bought two, but only told them about one. Figured on using the other one later; maybe with Tomdickandharry, maybe with some other guys, maybe alone. Didn't figure on Dottie getting us involved and us giving it to the press and the press making such a ruckus about it. So he lit out. Maybe if we'd played it low key, he wouldn't have vamoosed. Anyway, got as far as Amarillo and decided he'd better ditch the pill, it was too much of an M.O. to use it again, but he was just cussed enough that he wasn't going to totally waste it, so he put it in some woman's drink just because she didn't succumb to his charms. Then went on his way. Now we just have to catch up with him."

"We'll try. Get with the vic with those pictures of the hat and buckle. She may not be able to identify them, but if she says they're definitely not what she saw, that would keep us from a wild goose chase."

Dottie was still processing. Susan had called. They had her come down to the station to look at some pictures – of hats and belt buckles!?! *I didn't think it would do any good, but guess what? I not only picked out the type and color, but one hat and one buckle triggered my memory! I could see the man wearing the hat in the café.*

She could also see Dick wearing it. That fit with what Dick said. She didn't think it was a manufactured memory – she also saw two other guys, the ones Dick called Tom and Harry, and could give better descriptions of them and of George.

A mixed blessing. She felt like they were making progress, but now she had more faces in her nightmares. Mocking faces. Leering faces. Straining faces. Coming faces. Coming inside her. She was starting to understand what Sheri was talking about when she said how hard it would be to testify. How many different ways could she relive it? Sometimes she thought it would have been better to never know any of it, to go on knowing only that she had been in a café, that she woke up in the State forest, and that something had been done to her.

Which burns longer, a wax candle or a tallow candle? Neither, they both burn shorter. Which is better, to keep remembering what they did, or to not know anything? Neither. They're both worse. What is better is to never have been in that café, never to have met them, for the pharmacist never to have come to town. What is better is to live in a culture where…well, a different one than we have.

It never rains but it pours, Susan thought. *He didn't even tell me, didn't want too many people in the loop. The Chief brought in an FBI undercover agent – a man, it had to be a man – and he got the pharmacist.* So now both Dottie and the guy who sold the pills had identified George's hat and belt buckle and given descriptions. The pusher was being very cooperative. He was scared. He wanted a deal. *Fat chance,* Sheri thought.

He had described several of his customers. None of the descriptions were much help except George. He confirmed he sold George two pills. That was the standard buy. Minimum quantity to make it worth the risk, maximum quantity so the guy doesn't get sloppy using it too many times. Smart. Susan had never thought the guy was dumb. *So I was right on that piece. My theory is holding together so far.*

They got a subpoena for bank records. Found an ATM card issued on an Arizona bank that was used at four different ATMs in Stockbridge, Lenox, and Great Barrington on December 2, each time taking out all the cash the machine would allow. Didn't get used in Amarillo, but got used in Arkansas a couple of days before the lady got drugged and then in Winslow a few days later. It looked like George was travelling I-40, which took him right through Amarillo. So now they had a name and a pattern of motion. When the card was used again, they would be ready.

Wal-Mart. George always thought there was a certain class of people who gravitated to Wal-Mart as the employer of last resort. Never thought of himself as one of them, but he needed the cash. Just a couple of weeks, a month at the most, then he would move on. He was still confident enough that he had gotten away that he used his real social security card, driver's license, and passport. Turns out they had an opening in firearms. With his clean record and service experience, they couldn't wait to get him started. Monday morning he filled out his W-4 and direct deposit form and started selling AR-15s, Glocks, and replica Colt revolvers to the good people of Southern California.

Tuesday morning he was served with two arrest warrants. One out of Texas for reckless endangerment. One out of Massachusetts for first degree aggravated sexual assault. They would have caught up with him eventually with the social on his W-4, but the account number on the direct deposit form set off alarm bells almost immediately.

Texas was deferring to Massachusetts. They filed for extradition as a just-in-case. Just in case Massachusetts couldn't make the case to a California judge, Texas would be next in line. They needn't have bothered. George was back in the Berkshires before all the snow was melted on Crum Hill.

"State your name."

"Richard Henry Lee."

"And your current address?"

"Objection, Your Honor. Defense is willing to stipulate that Mr. Lee was brought here from a place of detention where he is serving time. We don't need to drag the details into this proceeding."

"Sustained."

"I withdraw the question. Mr. Lee, are you giving testimony in exchange for any considerations in your own case?"

"No, in fact I'm testifying against my will."

"How so?"

"I said when I confessed to my crime that I didn't want any plea deal or leniency, and that I wouldn't roll on my accomplices. I am only agreeing to testify today because you caught the defendant without my help."

"Do you waive your Fifth Amendment rights to not

self incriminate?"

"I'm not going to say anything today about my involvement that isn't substantially contained in the confession I have already given, that was the basis of my conviction and sentencing."

"Mr. Lee, will you tell us in your own words what happened on the evening of December 1, 2016 and the events leading up to it?"

I told this story already. It came out pretty much the same. When I said George told us he bought the roofies, the defense attorney objected as hearsay, so I just said George produced a pill and had Harry drop it in the victim's drink while George tried to dance with her. Focus on George's role. Stick to the facts. Keep the story consistent during cross. I did my best.

Testifying was harder than she imagined, and better than she thought it could be. Having finally dredged George up from her memory, she was ready to face him, but she wasn't ready for how his attitude hadn't really changed. Yes it was hard to tell her story. *But it's my story. It's part of me. I own it.* She was becoming proud of her survival. Still, it was hard to tell the story in front of all those strangers. She knew some of them were not going to hear it the right way, they were going to twist it and fold it and interpret it the same way the defense attorney was going to. She could see it in their eyes. She could see George smirking, but so could the jury, and that helped. She really struggled, but when she was done Dottie felt proud of herself for having gotten through it. It was a tough one, but it was a victory.

Cross was hell. Even though her turn came after Dick, so it was kind of tough for the defense to claim it had not been an unprovoked sexual assault, he kept trying. Poor guy, she guessed he had to, it was his job, and neither Dick's story nor George's attitude was helping. He must have been clutching at straws. *But I was the straw, and he was clutching at me, and I felt as violated as when they had physically clutched me.* "Didn't you dance with the defendant? Didn't

you encourage him? Why did you leave your coffee unat-
tended? Why were you in that café?' The DA redirected,
and gave her a chance to say she had changed cafés to get
away from the obnoxious element who had started fre-
quenting *Get Lit* – who she now recognized as George and
his cronies.

When it was all over, she really needed Sheri, and God
love her she was right there – just like she had promised in
the emergency room that she would be – with words of
encouragement and reassurance. So was Dottie's whole
support system.

22 DAN

I love to tell the story, T'will be my theme in Glory

This was getting nowhere. Several times Dan had had to just stand back and let the fur fly until people yelled themselves out. Conflict resolution wasn't a part of his background as a facilitator, and besides he didn't have the behavioral flexibility to be that kind of mediator. Knowing that about himself, and knowing what the potential was for this meeting, he probably should have brought in a colleague who was stronger in conflict, but the whole church was leery of outsiders. They were leery of him, but by now he had at least some credibility. Besides, the church had no money to hire a facilitator, and since he'd lost touch with the International Association of Facilitators, he didn't know anyone local that he could ask for a pro bono favor. Well, this tactic of letting things just burn out had always served him well – okay, adequately – before. But as he watched the latest brouhaha, he knew those were all excuses. He knew he'd blown it. He'd have to step up and identify a way forward.

As he listened to Mandy wind down her latest rant, Dan realized he'd seen this before. He'd dealt with Mandy's kind of resistance. Resistance is great, he heard his old mentor saying. Resistance is Energy. It beats the hell out of apathy. He just had to turn that energy to moving the group forward. It was time for The Question.

"Mandy, what are you afraid of?"

"I'm afraid of losing my Church."

silence

"How so? Say some more."

"I'm afraid that we're going to lose our grounding in the faith of our Fathers and in the Bible. I'm afraid it won't be the Church they struggled to build on the Rock of Jesus and that we've devoted our lives to keeping alive, and to keep pure to fundamental Christian teaching."

honor the silence

"I'm afraid that our church will be overrun by a certain element that flaunts their sin right under God's nose, that is not repentant for their sin but considers it an expression of love — their twisted, carnal idea of love. I'm afraid that the Bishop will get wind of what's going on here and come and take over our church and send us a new Pastor, not one as good as Pastor Allen. At least as good as Pastor Allen used to be. Pastor used to do exactly as told."

"By who?"

"By me! I mean, by all of us; Church Council, the diaconate, the elders, the established members, the church leaders. All of us."

"So you're afraid of losing control?"

"Yes! Darn right! This is my church and I know what we're supposed to do! I don't need any fancy 'discernment process.' I have the Bible and the *Book of Discipline.*"

"What about the Annual Conference act of non-compliance?"

"I was one of the 145 who voted against that, and I still think it's wrong!"

honor the silence

"What else?"

"What else do I need?"

"I mean what else are you afraid of?"

The silence was a little longer this time. Others raised their hands or started to speak, but Dan shushed them with a raised palm. When Mandy finally started up again, there was a catch to her voice. "I'm afraid that if I don't keep this church on the straight and narrow, that I'll be damned for it. If I get this wrong, if I'm not strong enough to stop it, I'll go straight to hell!" Mandy broke down sobbing. Donna got a tissue out of her purse, but Dan raised that "wait a minute" palm again, just as Alice put her hand on Donna's arm. They all waited through long seconds of Mandy's heaving and crying. Then, her voice cracking, Mandy said, "I'm afraid I'm going to hell if I don't get this right, and looking around this room at people who used to be my friends, seeing how much love is in this room, how much Christian caring, I'm not sure I'm right, I'm not sure of anything anymore, and I have to get it right."

Pastor Allen was the first to put arms around Mandy. Soon, everyone in room was moving towards her, towards the focus of love Mandy had become, getting as close as they could, and if they couldn't get close enough to lay on hands, they touched someone who was touching someone who was holding on to Mandy.

23 EASTER

Up from the grave he arose with a mighty triumph o'er his foes

Our scripture reading for today comes from the Gospel according to John, Chapter 20, verses 1 through 18. In this passage we read that Mary Magdalene was the first to find that the stone was rolled away from the tomb, but that John, the Gospel's purported author, was the first to discover the tomb was empty and Peter was the first to enter the empty tomb. Yet the greatest surprise is reserved for Mary.

One: Let us prepare ourselves for the Word of God as found in Holy Scripture.

Many: Our hearts and minds are open.

Early on the first day of the week, while it was still dark, Mary Magdalene came to the tomb and saw that the stone had been removed from the tomb. So she ran and went to Simon Peter and the other disciple, the one whom Jesus loved, and said to them, "They have taken the Lord out of the tomb, and we do not know where they have laid him." Then Peter and the other disciple set out and went toward the tomb. The two were running together, but the other disciple outran Peter and reached the tomb first. He bent down to look in and saw the linen wrappings lying there, but he did not go in. Then Simon Peter came, following him, and went into the tomb. He saw the linen wrappings lying there, and the cloth that had been on Jesus' head, not lying with the linen wrappings but rolled up in a place by itself. Then the other disciple, who reached the tomb first, also went in, and he saw and believed; for as yet they did not understand the scripture, that he must rise from the dead. Then the disciples returned to their homes. But Mary stood weeping outside the tomb. As she wept, she bent over to look into the tomb; and she saw two angels in white, sitting where the body of Jesus had been lying, one at the head and the other at the feet. They said to her, "Woman, why are you weeping?" She said to them, "They have taken away my Lord, and I do not know where they have laid him." When she had said this, she turned around and saw Jesus standing there, but she did not know that it was Jesus. Jesus said to her, "Woman, why are you weeping? Whom are you looking for?" Supposing him to be the gardener, she said to him, "Sir, if you have carried him away, tell me where you have laid him, and I will take him away." Jesus said to her, "Mary!" She turned and said to him in Hebrew, "Rabbouni!" (which means Teacher). Jesus said to her, "Do not hold on to me, because I have not yet ascended to the Father. But go to my brothers and say to them, 'I am ascending to my Father and your Father, to my God and your God.' " Mary Magdalene went and announced to the disciples, "I have seen the Lord"; and she told them that he had said these things to her.

May the lord guide our understanding of these words. Will you pray with me? May the words of my mouth and the meditation of our hearts be acceptable in thy sight, for you are our strength and our redeemer.

'Mary.' That was the word that caused the scales to fall from the eyes of Mary Magdalene who, according to John, was the first human being to be made aware that the divine human spark cannot be killed. The Christ, the Word, the Godhead, the Buddha, Brahmin, transcend life and death.

That which Jesus honored, tapped into, and lived out in a way that has been seen only a few times in human history is ultimately unquenchable. 'Mary.' Or in Spanish or Latin, 'Maria.' All the sounds of the world in a single word. I wonder if Stephen Sondheim knew what deep truth he was expressing when he penned that line.

Let's go back to what happened before this moment. In John, Mary Magdalene was the first to go to the tomb once the strictures of the Jewish Shabbat were lifted and the morning light allowed it. It was given to the faith and love of the feminine principle, to a woman among Jesus' followers, to be the first to the site of the event that would change forever the relationship between the human and the divine.

But Mary Magdalene mistrusted her role. She was a mere woman. A form of chattel. She could not own property. She could not even be a part of God's people, a partner in the covenant, because circumcision was the sign of the covenant and that was available only to males. Without a husband, father, or brother, only two professions were open to a woman, begging and prostitution, and since no one ever saw her begging they assumed the worst about Mary. So for all these reasons, when she realized something extraordinary had happened, she ran to get a man. She knew in the depths of her being – in the mind, heart, and soul that her culture had endowed her with over the course of a lifetime of brainwashing – that it was not a woman's place.

Jesus did not judge her without evidence And even if he had had evidence, Jesus was one of the first to understand that prostitution is not a crime of women against society, it is a crime of society against women. Jesus had tried for months to make her understand that her spark of divinity was no different than a man's, and she could probably say it was true, but in her core she did not accept it. Our beliefs, our stereotypes, our bigotry are deeply engrained and can take longer than a lifetime to unlearn. Her gut told her to go get the men.

But what happened when Peter and the other disciple whom Jesus loved arrived at the tomb? The other disciple got there first, and looked in, but he, too, mistrusted. He was not The Rock, so he did not enter. When Peter entered, he saw only the grave clothes. He did not – or could not – see the angels sitting in the tomb. The masculine principle, those concerned with the old covenant, the sex that for ten thousand years had been associated with domination, subjugation, and oppression, especially of women, would not serve for this revelation. They couldn't see the angels, and Jesus made himself scarce.

It was not until the men were gone and the angels had given tidings to Mary Magdalene that Jesus came to Mary. She did not recognize him at first – she took him to be the gardener. Maybe that was how he was dressed. After the soldiers cast lots for his clothes, he must have had to borrow something.

At one level it is not surprising that she did not recognize him. How many times have you not recognized someone, even someone you know well, when you saw them in a place where you do not expect to see them, maybe dressed in an unfamiliar way. Like someone from the office in workout clothes, or someone from your yoga class dressed for shopping. At one level, John is telling us that Mary Magdalene never expected to see Jesus alive again – certainly not in the garden, outside the tomb. John is making sure we know that this was a totally unexpected, unprecedented event.

But there is another level to this story, another lesson John wishes us to hear. It is the power of name. It was by speaking her name that Jesus struck Mary's core and made her realize how special she was. One of the ways in which men, in which patriarchal society, seek to rob women of their identity, their worth, is by the practice of expecting women to give up their names in marriage and take the name of their husband. In my mother's day, you weren't even Mrs. Rose Allen. You were Mrs. Jonathan Allen. For years women have bought into this, even to the extent that, when two women get married, they settle on one name for their new family. Otherwise they feel like they are disrespecting the married state they fought so hard for.

John said, 'No.' John included this detail, of Jesus revealing the mystery to a woman by the use of her name, to tell us that women have a right to a name, and to everything that goes with it. God named her and claimed her as God's own.

I have preached often from this pulpit about the shift in mythology that took place approximately 10,000 years ago, when one of about 100,000 cultures based on sustainability replaced their mythology with one that supported totalitarian agriculture, land ownership, and population increase to provide the slave labor needed for an economy of domination, subjugation, and oppression. What I have only occasionally touched upon is the role of women in this mythology, and the role of this mythology in the oppression of women for the last 10,000 years. Events of the last four and one half months have brought the issue to the forefront. We as a church are now a member congregation of the Reconciling Ministries Network, and I am proud not only of that decision but of your process. In some churches that decision is almost a foregone conclusion. In others it's never going to happen, either from deep rooted bias or from a lack of courage to even raise the issue. In the worst case, the vote pulls a congregation apart, and whichever way the majority votes, the church never recovers. But in this church, caring for one another, compassionate listening, and willingness to be with the Spirit led two opposing camps to unite in nearly unanimous support for this step. Next month I will be performing the first ever same-sex wedding in this church, and the first I have ever performed. While the decision to do that was made easier by the Annual Conference act of non-compliance, which promised no ecclesiastical trials, I could not even contemplate that decision without the outpouring of love from all of you.

But think back to the events that started our journey. It was a horrific crime. A crime against a woman of our church. A crime that we could not even conceive of happening to a man. That crime was a sexual assault of the most heinous nature.

Twenty-first century America is perhaps one of the best places and times to be a woman in the so-called civilized world since 10,000 B.C.E. That's not saying much. Every gain won is under constant assault by male chauvinists, religious fundamentalists, and social reactionaries. The safety of women is constantly compromised by a macho male culture that makes a woman nothing but a sexual object, sex nothing but a contest to be won by any means available, and rape a tool for proving power to yourself and others in a culture of power. It has to stop.

I did a little back-of-the-envelope figuring. Based on the best estimate of one in five college women being raped at least once in their college career and on the female population of our campuses, there must be an average of 20 to 30 rapes every week, just on the campuses of UMASS. Most of these are never reported. Almost none of them are covered in the press. Once in a while we get coverage of a sensational rape where the woman was walking across campus minding her business. Then the coverage is nonstop for a week. We never hear about the rapes where the victim indulged in what the male establishment press has decided to label 'risky' behavior. And we never hear prime time news stories on the statistics of unreported rape.

This is unacceptable. There needs to be a hue and cry from every woman and every man that this is not how we were meant to live. The life, sanity, sense of safety, freedom, and self-worth of the woman must be held up as seventy times seven times more valuable than the swimming career of the man. There should be a daily report of the number of reported rapes and the probable number of unreported rapes, just like during Viet Nam we got daily body counts.

And that is only the start. Rape is the inevitable conclusion of a hundred thousand assumptions about the role of women and what makes a man a man. Every one of those assumptions must be challenged on every level and every time they are encountered. The feminine principle, the ways of understanding the world that have been labelled as the anima or feminine nature, must be valued by all, and a man not in touch with his feminine side must be thought as ridiculous as one devoid of masculine values.

Anthropologists have looked back before this patriarchal society to see the matriarchal societies which they have imagined as the only other alternative. They didn't find them. What they found instead was evidence of societies of equality, where men and women had equal say in the running of the community. This is the natural human order.

It is this natural order that Jesus tapped into. He told Martha that the place of woman was not in the kitchen as a servant but with Mary at his feet, listening to The Word and becoming full partner in the new covenant; he told the crowd of men who wanted to stone the woman caught in adultery that their sins were at least as bad, if not worse, than simply calling into question the parentage of a child; and he began his entire ministry to the people of Samaria with the woman at the well.

Then Paul took it further. He said that in The Way there is no difference between men and women, rich and poor, north and south, circumcised and uncircumcised. He overthrew circumcision as the sign of the covenant and replaced it with baptism, an equal-opportunity experience.

So your take away, just in case you weren't listening to the rest of my sermon, is this. Equality, like excellence and forgiveness, takes practice. Equality is not an exception, something reserved for the big issues like rape and pay equity. It is a habit of thought.

In the words of Joss Whedon, 'Equality is not a concept. It's not something we should be striving for. It's a necessity. Equality is like gravity, we need it to stand on this earth as men and women, and the misogyny that is in every culture is not a true part of the human condition.'

May it be so.

24 APRIL COME SHE WILL

For wherever two or more of you are gathered in his name
There is love, there is love

I Glenda, the Glenda you see before you, without pretense or hidden agendas,

Take you Dottie, not the Dottie of my expectations or imagination but the Dottie you actually are, and any Dottie you may become,

To be my lawfully wedded wife. We've made a lot of commitments to each other. Now we wrap those promises up in one big, beautiful package, and give it the force of law, and make it holy by promising before God and these witnesses. And what are those promises?

To have and to hold. I promise to hold you in friendship, in love, and in passion. I promise to hold on to you when you need support, and I promise to hold on to you when I need support.

In good times and in bad, because you make the good times worthwhile and the bad times better.

For richer and for poorer, and for that in between place where we will probably find ourselves most of the time. When we have enough money to buy anything we want but not enough money to buy everything we want, I promise to remember that our commitments to each other, to God, and to the stewardship of God's bounty are more important than the things we have or the things we don't have.

In sickness and in health. When you are sick, I will nurse you, and when I am sick, I will try to be a good patient.

Till death do us part. The final transition of this life has a beauty all its own. I promise to stick around to share that beauty, whichever side I'm on.

And I know that I can only keep these promises if they find favor with and help from the Universal Absolute that has gifted us with our love. Amen

Glenda, you are my sun and my moon, my morning and my evening, my coming and my going, my rising and my lying down. You are my wife and my husband, my partner and my lover. I Dottie cleave to you Glenda through whatever life throws at us for as long as we draw breath, for you are my breath and the beat of my heart.

Place the rings on each other's fingers and repeat after me. 'With this ring, I give you my heart. From this day forward, you shall not walk alone. May my arms be your home.'

The wedding took place in Third Methodist Church, and Pastor Allen officiated. Pastor was not taking as big a chance on being turned in to Annual Conference for performing an illegal marriage, not since last summer's act of non-compliance, where the New England Annual Conference voted to allow openly homosexual ministers to be ordained and ended the threat of ecclesiastical trials. The way the church had unified around the resolution to join the Reconciling Ministries Network, it didn't seem likely that anyone would have turned Pastor in anyway.

The attendants came down the central aisle. Mary's youngest was the ring bearer, and Donna's youngest was the flower girl. They thought for a long time about not being so gender specific, but some people are only ready for just so much change.

Next were the bridesmaids, Donna, Maria, and Juanita. Then the best man and the matron of honor together. Alice served as matron of honor to both of them, and Dave was their joint best man. Then, to Wagner's Wedding March from Lohengrin, the one everyone knows as 'Here Comes the Bride,' Glenda and Dottie came down opposite side aisles, accompanied by the persons they chose to give them away. Mary gave away Dottie, and Mandy gave away Glenda. It's a tossup as to who was more surprised, Mandy when Glenda asked her or Glenda when Mandy accepted – or the church when Mandy and Glenda came down the side aisle. Mandy even gave her a kiss as she turned her over to Dottie.

There was the welcome. There was the charge. There was the 'If any can show reason…' and everyone held their breath, but with Mandy giving away one of the brides, who was left to object? There were the vows. There was the exchanging of rings. After the 'I now pronounce you…' there was the kiss. There was probably some discomfort when they kissed, but even the uncomfortable ones thought, 'In for a Penny, in for a Pound.' Heterosexual couples had been kissing during the passing of the peace for years. Not like Glenda and Dottie kissed, of course. This was their first kiss as a married couple and they were going to make it memorable. Then, holding tightly to each other's arm, they marched down the center aisle to the Grand March from Tannhäuser.

The reception was in the church basement. The whole church was there, along with Glenda's sister and most of the staff of the Rock. There were even a few of the most loyal customers of the Ferguson. The whole staff of the Fergie had been in the wedding party.

The honeymoon was short – from the Saturday after Easter until the next Tuesday. Some said it was because they had been together so long already. Some said it was because, when you live in the Berkshires year 'round, who needs to go away on a honeymoon? But the real reason was that the off season was almost over. Glenda really had to get back to the bed and breakfast. They were in good shape, but they had to be on top of their game now. All hands on deck, and time to start to looking for the high school kids who would be the extra housekeepers on Tanglewood weekends. This was definitely *not* the year when Glenda would be selling, but she felt good, they all felt good, knowing what Dave, Maria, and Juanita could do when asked. Maybe with another junior housekeeper, she could semi-retire. There were all kinds of possibilities.

EPILOGUE

The autumn winds blow chilly and cold.
September I'll remember.

Dottie got back to the museum full time. She can only go there in her new outfits. They make her feel like a different woman from the one who was attacked.

She has started presenting a session on safety in public places at the *True Colors Conference*. It's a perennial favorite, but mostly with parents and adult allies. The youth think they have nothing to worry about – until it happens to them. Dottie has ambivalent feelings about the session. She still wishes she could be changing society so that her session wasn't needed. She tweets annually: 'When she can't do what she wants, go where she wants, and wear what she wants, the rape has already started. #stoprape'

Dottie still has nightmares, and sometimes being with Glenda snaps her back to waking up half naked and half frozen. That's when Glenda holds her the tightest.

George got a reduced sentence for turning in Tom and Harry. Tom and Harry's lawyers negotiated plea deals; there were no more trials, no more confrontations, no more courtroom traumas, no more costly victories.

Dick is still in prison. He doesn't get any visitors anymore. His father never saw him again after he made his confession.

His mother defied her husband. A devout person will tell you that, at its purest, a mother's love is the best example we have on Earth of what the love of God is like. Even an atheist will tell you that a mother's love is the source of the human archetype of selfless love for which God became a metaphor. Dick's mother visited him every month until her death. She always came on a Thursday, and she always wore black.

#ThursdaysinBlack towards a world without rape and violence against women.

ABOUT THE AUTHOR

E.S "Ned" Ruete is an author, speaker, group facilitator, women's rights activist, LGBTQIPA+ ally, lay preacher, guitar picker, and business analyst. He is the author of *Seeking God: Finding God's both/and in an either/or world* and *Lead Your Group to Success: A Meeting Leader's Primer.*

Now retired, Ned lives in Niantic, Connecticut with his second wife. He continues to offer *pro bono* group facilitation and facilitation training to schools, churches, community groups and not-for-profit organizations. He has led strategic planning retreats for United Action Connecticut (UACT), Fiddleheads Food Co-op, and ReNew London. He is actively involved in LGBTQIPA+ advocacy and annually attends and presents sessions at the *True Colors Conference.* He is a member of the International Association of Facilitators (IAF) and formerly served on the Association Coordinating Team (ACT, the IAF Board of Directors). He was associate editor of *Group Facilitation: A Research and Applications Journal* and has contributed articles to *Group Facilitation, The Facilitator,* and other publications on group facilitation and management consulting.

Off Season is Mr. Ruete's first fiction work.